P9-CLV-140

Revision: Peter McCambridge
Proofreading: Daniel J. Rowe, David Warriner, Elizabeth West
Book design: Folio infographie
Cover & logo: Maison 1608 by Solisco
Fiction editor: Peter McCambridge

Originally published under the title *Les bains électriques* by La Mèche, une division du Groupe d'édition la courte échelle inc., 2018 (Montréal, Québec)

ISBN 978-1-77186-214-1 pbk; 978-1-77186-215-8 epub; 978-1-77186-216-5 pdf

Legal Deposit, 2nd quarter 2020
Bibliothèque et Archives nationales du Québec
Library and Archives Canada

Published by QC Fiction, an imprint of Baraka Books
Printed and bound in Québec

TRADE DISTRIBUTION & RETURNS

Canada - UTP Distribution: UTPdistribution.com

United States & World - Independent Publishers Group: IPGbook.com

We acknowledge the financial support for translation and promotion of the Société de développement des entreprises culturelles (SODEC), the Government of Québec tax credit for book publishing administered by SODEC, the Government of Canada, and the Canada Council for the Arts.

Financé par le gouvernement du Canada
Funded by the Government of Canada | Canada

Jean-Michel Fortier

THE ELECTRIC BATHS

Translated from the French by
Katherine Hastings

QC FICTION

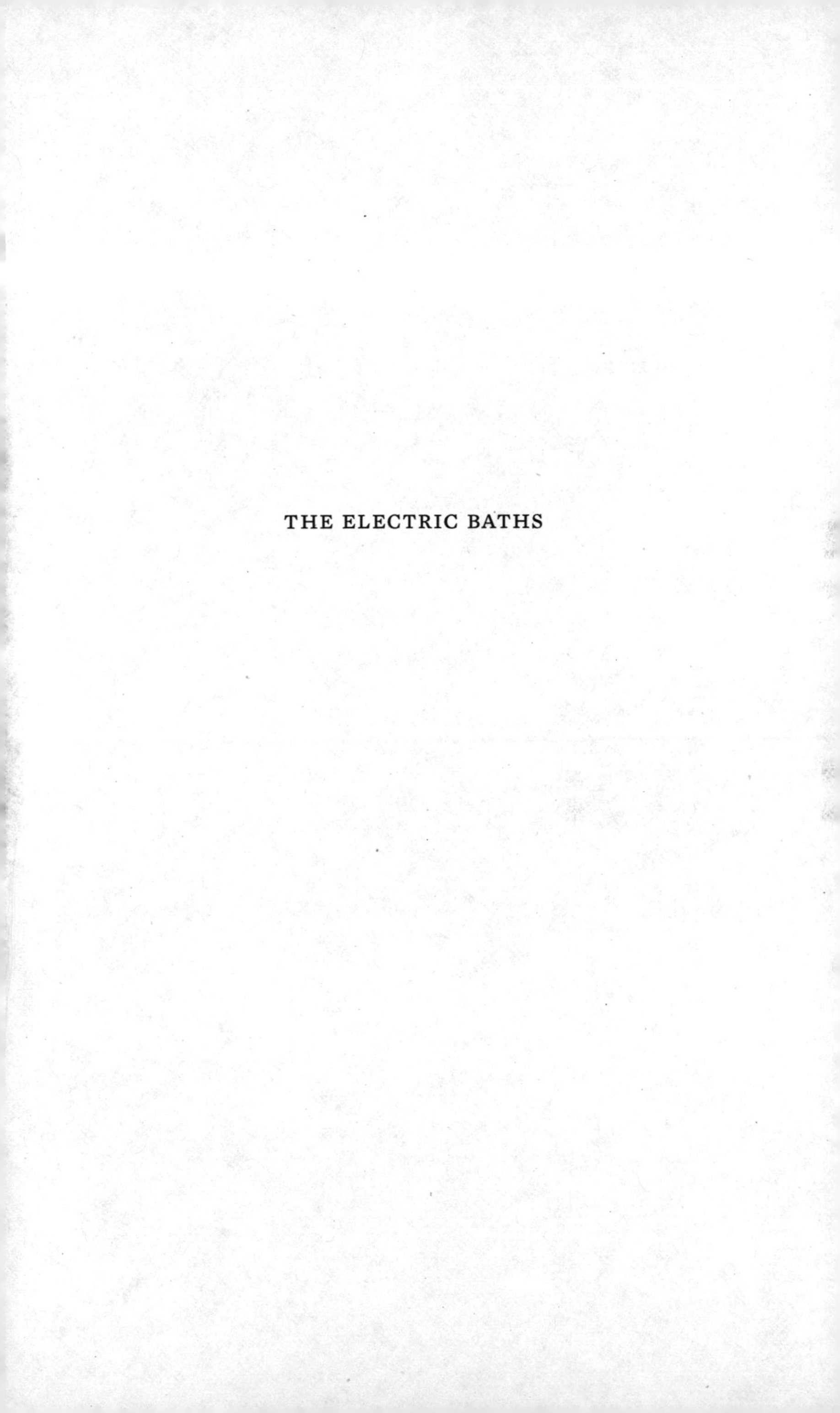

THE ELECTRIC BATHS

"Just look how Madame loves Monsieur!
You see, she's crying..."

— Anne Hébert, *Kamouraska*
(translated by Norman Shapiro)

1

“MY HEART HAS STOPPED.”

“Relax, it’ll start up again.”

Old Mr. Roux used to walk past Renée’s window every morning on his way to the store, but he never spoke to her. He always hurried by, the wind billowing in his overcoat like the sails of a ship, pulling and pushing him this way and that along the sidewalk, as if an invisible gendarme had arrested him and was matching his stride and dragging him along by his arm.

Renée was watering her pansies. She wouldn’t have looked up from her window box if Old Roux hadn’t altered course that morning and come over to stick his nose in her flowers, a gleeful look on his face.

"Louise is back, Miss Lepine."

"What did you say?"

All she could see of the man were the liver spots dotting his skull; even his eyes were hidden behind the purple pansy blossoms. He cackled, senile.

"I said, Louise is back."

Renée set down her watering can, closed her eyes, took a deep breath as the wind filled Old Roux's sleeves, then breathed out as they deflated.

"My heart has stopped."

"Relax, it'll start up again."

He was still smiling as he said, "What a shock. Indeed, what a shock! Give my greetings to the pensioner," then, taking her hand as you might your sister's, "The years may pass, but sentiments remain," and off he went, looking for all the world like a kite carried off in a gust of wind.

Renée Lepine had been called all kinds of names in her time, but only a crazy man—or woman—would say she was sentimental. And Old Roux was crazy. As he continued on his way, his overcoat flapping, she heard her own words once again, "My heart has stopped," and she was ashamed at having exposed herself so, even to him. She wanted to run after him and shake him like a plum tree to dislodge those words—"My heart has stopped"—from his ears; she would have gathered them up, stuffed them in her pocket, and sewed it up three times over if she could.

The Louise in question had been gone for the past thirteen years, and it was the first time she'd been back to the village. Renée had repeated this story to herself over and again, and had eventually handpicked and placed each word just as you would decorate a parlour, a parlour that no one ever uses:

"One day a circus came to town. It was led by a fat man with a moustache who always wore a blue kepi, and he asked Louise to join them. She would start out shovelling elephant dung while he taught her to do acrobatics. Her body was perfectly proportioned for standing with one leg on one horse and the other on a second, arms stretched out like a swirling star (that's how he put it: like a little, white swirling star), and she liked to imagine herself as a star balanced on the ponies' backs; it helped her to forget the elephant and its dung.

Back then I worked at the village store, and Louise came to see me at the counter to tell me she was leaving. We waved goodbye to each other as the circus made its way down the main street with its elephant, its hand-painted wagons (red with yellow stars)—Renée would always let out a little laugh at this point—the plump ringmaster in his hat, and Louise sitting beside him wearing a dress that looked as if it were about to slide off her narrow shoulders.

After that, the months went by, one after the other. Louise would sometimes write about the cities and the shows. A handful of letters in thirteen years is all I have left of her and our years of companionship. As for the rest, well, that's all I know."

Here's the rest: the man in the kepi eventually revealed his true, unsavory motives and Louise set him straight, no thank you, but if she wanted to perform in the circus, she would have to bend to his wishes, that was the way it was, so she contented herself with shovelling dung. The elephant became her friend, and she never performed on horseback, but the circus continued to travel far and wide, and one December day it pulled into a port town.

Louise managed to get the afternoon off and found a cinema where *Fantômas* was playing. She'd never been to the movies before, and while she was waiting in line to buy a ticket, another rotund man, this one in a black hat, came up to her and asked her to join him and his theatre troupe. They were about to board a ship to the Old World to perform there, and one of their actresses had just run off with a soldier to the land of the maharajas. They needed to replace her, not with just any girl, but with Louise, something to do with proportions and costumes. They needed Louise right away to replace the actress with the very same measurements. She agreed, but asked that she be allowed to watch the film first; it was her day off, after all. The man in the hat said where they were going, she'd be able to watch as many movies as she wanted. No, she wanted to watch this one, now. He sat with her and they watched it together, but as soon as it was over, they had to go because the ship wouldn't wait. She thought of her elephant and the dung; she didn't give a second thought to the piggish man in the blue kepi, and she climbed aboard the ship.

There, she met the other members of the troupe: a lady as short and stout as a deck of cards; a handsome, fine-featured man who, she immediately guessed, she would be playing opposite; a tall clown with rubbery cheeks;

and another man, somewhat grey and uncouth, but very versatile. The director of the troupe, the man in the black hat, had her practice her lines, and reassured her: she may never have acted before, but all she had to do was to look straight out at the audience, say her lines in a nice loud voice, and be feeble when her partner was strong.

During the crossing she thought about writing to Renée, but she shared a cabin with the stout actress, who was always peering over her shoulder, criticizing her scrawl, her style, her syntax, so that, in the end, Louise gave up on the idea.

The troupe docked in Cherbourg and it rained for two whole months. The shabby theatre where they performed was rarely full, but for Louise, it was a learning experience, and to her surprise, neither her stage partner, nor the man in the black hat, nor the clown, nor even the plain-looking man behaved inappropriately towards her.

After six months in Cherbourg, they packed up and headed to Paris where, according to the director, "the audiences would kiss their feet." Louise was starting to get the hang of the accent which, according to the others, really improved her acting and gave her the air of a real actress. In Paris, the troupe immediately felt at home, taking up residence at the Théâtre de l'Ambigu-Comique, on what was known to all as the Boulevard du Crime. The melodramas they performed there were based on grisly actual events—a theme that suited them well, especially the versatile actor, who always shone in the role of sadist.

On their arrival in Paris, the troupe director decided to make it official and sign Louise to a contract, as she attracted audiences, especially in the role of the starving waif whose baby is snatched and sold off, and it was at the moment he was drawing up said contract binding the young woman to the troupe for another year that she became Louisa Louis, because the barrister turned to her and said:

"Name?"

"Louise Beurre," she replied.

"Beurre as in butter, as in, what you put in the butter dish?"

"Yes, like in a butter dish."

The troupe director stepped in at that point because there was obviously no way Louise Beurre could perform at the Théâtre de l'Ambigu-Comique; she would have to be Louise

Beringer or Louisette Bernari, or some mysterious-sounding name, perhaps something with an Oriental ring to it. He planned to put her on the posters, to make her the star of the troupe. She realized she would need a name, a proper name, not too common, yet not too foreign either (that wouldn't do) so she suggested Louisa Louis, which the two men found amusing—amusing and refreshing—and so she signed Louisa Louis.

When she proudly told the others about her new name, the Queen of Clubs asked:

"Was your name really Louise Beurre? *Beurre* as in butter in a churner?"

"No, not like in a churner; like in a butter dish. *Quand même!*"

The months in Paris were tough for Louisa Louis, because the public demanded quality: they didn't like it when she wrinkled her nose when she laughed (too Béatrix Dussane), and she couldn't crane her neck either (too Réjane). It was all part of her education as an actress, the troupe director explained.

She saw lots of films in Paris, and was especially fond of Louis Feuillade's silent series *Les Vampires.* One evening at the theatre, the boxy lady remarked that Mr. Feuillade himself was in the audience, at the far corner of the hall.

Louisa's pulse quickened, and she neither wrinkled her nose nor craned her neck onstage that night, except once, to see if she could spot the famous director. While he wasn't wearing a hat, she dreamed nonetheless that he would be the third man to ask her to follow him, to play in a film. But, alas, the only woman he hired to star in his films in those days was Musidora, a well-established actress.

Louise eventually adopted airs of her own, a pout and several gestures that became her trademark as an actress: she would press her index and middle fingers together when pointing, and became known for it. She was sure the troupe would make its breakthrough soon enough and take her to Brussels, Warsaw, St. Petersburg, but the months passed and still nothing changed.

In the end she grew fed up with the troupe, especially with the other actress, who accused her of stealing her corsets. One fine evening after a performance, Louise left the theatre through the back entrance, her bag under her arm, crossed the Rive Gauche, and disappeared from view altogether. Until she turned up in her village, ten years later.

Renée Lepine spent the evening sewing buttons on a frock coat, but like all the other chores she'd done that day, this one still didn't help her forget Old Roux's visit and his news, nor the harsh words of Marquette the pensioner, who had called out to Renée as she came in: "I hear Louise Beurre was a flop in Paris! A big, buttery flop! Apparently, she's been back for a week. She's been hiding out at the home of the widow Clot!"

Louise's secret return caused Renée more anguish than her ten years of silence. "She's been back for a week: imagine all the things one has time to do in a week!" A letter could travel from one end of the country to the other in a week. If she'd come back without saying a word because she wanted to surprise me, that would have been one thing. But no, she's here, only three streets over, and it's as if she were still across the ocean." Her body instinctively sought out a bed on which to collapse until her sadness subsided. Her gammy leg, the result of contracting polio at the age of twelve, seemed to get worse, no doubt as punishment for her cowardice and spinelessness. Her thoughts turned to the bravest person she knew, wise Celeste, who would surely advise her to go and visit her old friend: "You know she's staying with the widow Clot. Why don't you go and see her? She'd like that!"

Renée thought, too, about a novel she'd read in which the heroine suffers a fall that leaves her crippled and ugly, yet merciful and grateful at the same time. She wished she could believe in something that would help her accept the disappointments in her life. But she merely ended up sobbing to the point of exhaustion.

An hour later, the pensioner pushed open the front door, dragging by the arm a fat, wriggling creature. The hem of her dress hung so low it had caught on the tongue of her boots, and she shuffled forward in the dark, sniffling and wiping her nose on the back of her hand.

"Quiet, Bella!"

"I can't see anything, Armand."

She cackled as she dragged her heavy boots across the varnished floor.

Renée, hands folded under her chin, back wedged between two bedsprings, feet pointing towards the ceiling like a mummy, struggled to block out her day.

Above her, a sand-coloured spider was weaving its web between two branches of the chandelier. Its work complete, the spider slowly descended along its thread towards Renée's half-moon face. But a draft suddenly set the web a-shimmer, and the spider opted instead to climb back up to its hideaway.

It was because of Bella Webb, the pensioner's late-night guest, who had accidentally cracked open the bedroom door, mistaking it for the lavatory.

2

AS BELLA PULLED THE BEDROOM DOOR closed and continued down the hallway, Renée Lepine felt herself falling.

It was all peaks and cliffs. She couldn't see herself. She moved forward, floating between the rocks. No trees, no ocean, no sky, but it wasn't a cave. She avoided the rocky cones that spiked up beneath her feet, that pressed down from above; she was afraid to brush up against them.

And in the distance, an impasse where the ground met the ceiling.

Up above, the yellow spider swung back and forth, tracing the arc of a pendulum.

Renée woke, sat up, and, on the wooden slats at the foot of her bed, her gaze tripped over a grey pebble, partly illuminated by the light of the moon. Its shiny surface filled her eyes until it became a photograph of the pebble, a close-up of the pebble, the detail of the pebble, the infinite pores of the pebble that eclipsed the room, the pensioner's house, the whole county.

She felt the pebble in her mouth, hard and smooth, and was afraid she would bite down on it and break her teeth.

Then, the pebble penetrated deep inside her. Her tongue, her nostrils, her forehead turned to stone. In her veins there was sand; she was calcifying. She knew there were spikes protruding from her ears. She didn't want to break them, she didn't want to fracture her skull, she felt her head turn crumbly. Slowly, trembling, trembling at the thought of brushing against the sharp spikes that had sprung up, she brought her hands towards her face and gently probed her neck and the back of her head. She wanted to do more, but she couldn't.

And she held her head in her hands, mouth agape, eyes unfocussed, and she felt nothing, but she knew, oh she knew, they were there, those spikes, that stone in her brain, and it was almost worse not feeling anything, seeing only that hard, shiny pebble that would fill her palm the way it was filling her mind, growing ever bigger, but that was visible only in her eyes, only in the lunar white that illuminated its violent inertia on the wooden floor, where at last she fell, consumed by the tingling sensation of knowing she was in her dream but unable to escape it without screaming.

3

BELLA WEBB WAS SMILING broadly when she woke, but it was just the sun. The pensioner had left hours earlier. He was probably roaming around the village, or settling some business in his office, or reading the newspaper.

She knew the drill. She had to walk quietly. Her dress was rumpled practically from top to bottom. Turn left down the hallway and go out the back. Avoid bumping into Renée, though the pensioner had assured her she often got up late, that she wasn't the ideal servant, that he'd taken her on only out of pity, charity and all that. He would much prefer that she, Bella, take her place.

When she stepped outside, she stretched languorously. A trickle of rainwater ran alongside the back alley. Near the middle of the sloped lane, a pile of leaves blocked the flow, forming a puddle. The water slowly pooled. The puddle grew larger.

Bella stood there a moment, waiting until the water finally made its way around the dam and continued on down the lane. And when it did, she wiped her nose on the back of her hand and headed off in the opposite direction.

The door of the village store jammed at the top when Bella tried to push it open.

"Margot!"

If Margot was there, she wasn't answering. Bella slipped her arm through the crack, thumped on the frame, and managed to shove the door open.

"Margot!" she called again.

An old biddy in a stained dress, her petticoat drooping beneath the hem, suddenly appeared from behind a pile of boxes, causing Bella to start. It was Celeste, the sort of woman who looked as though she might shatter at a mere touch. Surprised to hear Bella Webb's booming voice, Celeste grumbled under her breath. She preferred Margot, a good and simple woman, to gloomy Bella, but she was philosophical about such matters, and soon enough recovered her toothy but radiant smile, and asked:

"Where's the boss? Isn't she coming?"

Bella hadn't the slightest idea. She was just as surprised, as she'd been expecting to find Margot there and to tell her all about the previous night. But the boss had sent her eldest boy very early that morning to tell Celeste she'd be needing her in the store today. The two employees shrugged their shoulders.

"Ah well, that's unlike her. But still, it's better than in Renée's day."

Renée would have vigorously defended herself had she been awake, but the absent party is always to blame, and Bella sniggered.

"Renée—hah!—it was a miracle if she showed up to work every other day!"

"And even then, she'd be an hour late!"

The two women shared a laugh as they began sweeping the floor, with Celeste almost managing to swallow her distaste for strapping Bella, who had a tendency to stay out late after dark.

The first customer of the day showed up at nine o'clock, but he too struggled with the jammed door, and Celeste rushed to help him while Bella shouted, "It's the wood that's swollen," and then again, to be sure he'd heard: "It's the wood that's swollen." She clasped her hands behind her back and shifted from one foot to the other, like a prize fighter.

The customer wanted to buy some rope, a long length of rope for this and that, he explained, with a great many words and much blinking of the eyes. Celeste enjoyed serving customers, and she sold the man his rope while Bella wiped down the counter and shelves with a rag.

He left clutching his purchase in both hands, a satisfied look on his face.

"What's he going to do with that?"

Celeste turned, distracted.

"What's he going to do with that?" Bella repeated.

"He explained, but I'm not sure I quite understood. Maybe he's a farmer. I've never seen him around."

"Neither have I. A rather strange fellow. Do you think he plans to hang himself?"

"He seemed perfectly alright. We can't possibly know everyone who comes in. Hang himself? Really! Don't say that!"

The two women sat down on their stools, one at either end of the counter, in a long but comfortable silence. They created a strange imbalance in the store that seemed to lean more towards Bella;

that actually *did* lean towards Bella, come to think of it, thanks to the crooked floor.

"Do you think he's rich? The man with the rope—is he rich, do you think?"

Celeste rolled her eyes.

"What difference does it make?"

"To you, absolutely none, I know that much!"

Celeste had grown up on a large plot of land to the north, near the water, that her father had bequeathed to his three sons upon his death. To his sole daughter he passed down only an obsession with work and its rewards. She had worked in the village for twenty years, and in the store for ten of those, but she lived on a country lane off the main road that led to the grand estate of Spencer Wood, the Jewish manor house. She lived with her husband, a cripple, in a house that was long, very long, surrounded by ash trees that hung over it like a sunshade. Between the store and Spencer Wood, Celeste did all kinds of jobs: in the daytime, she could be found behind the counter of the village store, and in the evenings or on her days off, she would offer her services to the masters of the estate, washing windows, scrubbing floors, sweeping chimneys, picking horses' hoofs, gardening, shovelling. She would roll up her sleeves and set to work, the veins in her arms bulging. Her forehead was permanently furrowed with one deep line. She was as strong and sturdy as a workhorse, and no task was beneath her. "All work is noble," she often said.

"Louise Beurre is back from her travels."

Bella Webb cocked her head.

"Is that so?"

Celeste had only mentioned it in passing, not realizing that Bella was lapping up her every word.

"Old Mr. Roux told me she's staying with the widow Clot. And he told Renée, and she looked distressed."

"Distressed?"

"Yes, you know, distressed."

Bella frowned in disgust:

"So unnatural..."

Celeste said, in a philosophical tone:

"You can't stop a heart from loving."

The second customer of the day pushed on the door, which jammed for the third time. Bella gave the wedged corner a good shove and welcomed the visitor with an effusive smile; he said he needed needles and thread and some cotton. "Ah yes, and some rat poison," he said.

He was served by Bella, all smiles and fawning, as obsequious as can be.

4

"GINETTE'S CONFINED TO HER BED. She threw her back out tightening a nut on a machine, on some equipment her husband uses for the hay. She's down for the count, so we won't be enough to play belote. I thought about inviting Louise Beurre—did you know she goes by Louisa Louis now?—until I remembered you and she had a falling out, what was it about again? I can't remember for the life of me; it was thirteen years ago, after all. Anyway, then I thought maybe the widow Clot, but since Louise is rooming there, she would surely find out and wouldn't take it well, you know what women are like, then I thought perhaps Basil could be the fourth hand, but he's such a slowpoke, and

I for one didn't feel like spending the evening over at Celeste's in the back of beyond, and getting home at all hours. And, you know, Friday is belote night, after all, and players are hard to come by, it seems, so I invited Renée."

Such a long-winded explanation just for the tanned, flat face and big black eyes of Bella Webb, who was cradling an elephantine cat in her arms, rubbing her beefy hand between its ears, while the feline stretched its neck and closed its eyes, all the better to enjoy her caress.

"I thought you and Renée weren't on speaking terms."

Bella spoke as she gazed into the eyes of the cat, holding it up to her face, her hands under its front legs the way you'd hold a baby to get it to gurgle and smile. Margot picked at a drop of dried wax on the table, her expression swinging from contrite to apologetic.

"Oh no, not at all. No. We say our hellos when we see one another. You know I can't stand a quarrel; before you know it, it's made the rounds and back."

Bella wasn't exactly sure what Margot meant by that, but she was perfectly sure what she was about to say next:

"Celeste and I aren't crazy about Renée, you know."

"Really? Celeste too? Well, I'm afraid you'll just have to accept the fact, with Ginette out of action and Louise... would you have preferred Louise? I would think not, if you had to choose between Louise and her grand airs and Renée; well sure, she's a real worrywart and all, but still, I'd rather play cards with her. What on earth would you talk about with that other woman? Here she is, back from the Old World with all her tales of acrobats and whatnot; Old Roux says she really flopped in Paris, so frankly, for our belote night, I can't imagine what we'd have talked about—hats, ribbons, and sealing wax?"

She shook her head like someone emerging from a daydream, a look on her face as if she wondered why in heaven's name she'd been talking about sealing wax, and immediately lost her train of thought.

Margot's cat batted the air with its big paws, still suspended between Bella's hands, while she continued to stare into its eyes and said:

"We could always play salad instead. You can play it with three. We could skip belote for once."

Margot brushed away a few imaginary specks of dust from the table, her week had been difficult enough as it was, the store's profits were rarely to her satisfaction. So what with that and the demands of Bella Webb, "No thank you, I'll pass." Just then someone knocked at the door and in came Celeste together with Renée Lepine, who she'd met on the way. "I bumped into Renée in the street, and what a surprise to learn that we were going to the same place—a pleasant surprise, all the same."

A strange tableau: the oil lamp with its dull copper sheen, the messy kitchen, the wobbly table, Bella to the right of Renée, the cat still in her grip, Celeste looking content, her arms crossed over her apron, and Margot, looking annoyed as she cut the deck and dealt the cards.

They'd taken out the black kings to form the teams: Margot with Renée, Celeste with Bella. Fortunately!

The game held their full attention for the better part of an hour, especially Renée, who hadn't played cards for years and had a hard time remembering all the rules, but nonetheless, she played at a decent pace, despite the occasional comment by Bella Webb, who noted every little mistake in an even tone, her eyes never straying from her hand.

They made it to two thousand points before finally declaring Bella and Celeste the winners, although by only a slim margin. Celeste would never take the trump card, which annoyed Bella no end, as she had no qualms about taking, even if it was only to confound the others; she would take the card with nothing but a nine, always relying on her partner to follow with a Jack (she liked to live dangerously). Margot couldn't care less about winning, she only wanted to keep Bella happy. As for Renée, she'd come along simply for the distraction, but as the evening wore on, she grew increasingly keen to give Bella a sound thrashing. They started in on another round, this time with Renée and Celeste on one team, and Bella and Margot on the other.

This time Renée played more confidently, and since her partner was always there to back her up, they won, even though Celeste kept forgetting to say "belote" and "rebelote." Bella Webb made an angry remark to Margot when they lost, which whet her appetite for a cruel jab, and she continued:

"What about that Louise Beurre? What a character! Or, Louisa Louis, I should say."

Renée sat up straighter in her chair.

"She's back from her gallivanting. Apparently, she's staying at the widow Clot's house. What in the world could have happened that she would suddenly just show up like that, after thirteen years?"

Celeste and Margot cringed as Bella Webb rambled on, her hands plunged into the cat's fur. "They say she married a rich man over there, a duke, no less. And that she was unable to bear him a child, so he plonked her on a boat and found himself another woman. All expenses paid, and an allowance to boot!"

"You know, Bella, I really have no interest in such tittle-tattle."

In reality, the words struck Renée to the core, but since she was a woman with no one to rely on but herself, she did her utmost to turn a deaf ear to the rumours, to stem the wave of anxiety she felt rising within.

Celeste suggested they play a third round, but by that time they were all yawning, except for Renée, who was stung by Bella's words, her heart pounding. The women collected their hats and headed for home. Luckily, Bella and Celeste went off in the same direction, vigorous and confident, while Renée hobbled off the other way.

5

"LOUISE! Louise Beurre!"

The widow Clot had managed to get her foot stuck in the ash bucket and couldn't work it loose.

"Louise!"

She'd been crying wolf for a while, but Louise Beurre had left her room early that morning to go for a walk before the whole village awoke and someone—namely, Renée Lepine—bumped into her on the main street. Contrary to the rumours making the rounds, Louise had returned without a penny to her name and with no allowance. And after enduring a week of the widow Clot's salty cooking, she was off to find alternate lodgings. Like any self-respecting gossipmonger, Old

Mr. Roux, who'd been peddling news of Louise's "wanderings" up and down the county—as she was well aware—nonetheless deserved credit for providing her with the latest chitchat from round about.

"I hear they're looking for help at Spencer Wood."

"Is that so? What kind of help?"

"Something to do with Turkish baths, I believe it is."

"Turkish baths?" she repeated in surprise.

And so it was that around ten o'clock that morning, Louise Beurre—known in the fanciest French theatres as Louisa Louis, and still adorned in fabrics far too lustrous for the county—knocked at the door of Spencer Wood. It opened with a rasping sound to reveal a girl of about eleven or twelve wearing a dusky pink dress, her hair like a towering pile of fluff.

"Lisa Rosenberg."

The child held out her right hand, her left still gripping the door handle. Louise, taken aback, shook it feebly.

"And you are...?"

The girl's high-pitched voice demanded a precise answer, as if it were a test. Louise hesitated a moment, then the bangles she'd bought in Montmartre jangled, as if to provide the answer:

"Louisa Louis."

Lisa Rosenberg nodded, which Louise took to mean "Ah, very good, indeed, a very good name."

"And you would like...?"

Louise started a little. "I would like," she struggled to say what exactly it was she would like, but she had to say something:

"I'm looking for work."

"I'm not the one in charge of that."

Lisa replied without hesitation. While motioning Louise to enter the house, she pushed aside a large panting dog that was attempting to jump up on the visitor.

"My mother selects her employees herself."

Louise pushed up the bangles that had slid down her arm:

"Ah, your mother?"

"Do you know who my mother is?"

The child was so poised that Louise Beurre felt as insipid as she had the day the man in the kepi had led her away.

"My mother is Sarah Rosenberg."

Visibly bursting with pride, she might just as well have announced that her mother was the Queen of Sheba. Then, since nothing else appeared forthcoming, and she was feeling more and more uncomfortable, Louise asked if she might meet Madam Rosenberg, and Lisa led her off to a bright little parlour. Louise sat down on the straightest chair she could find. The furniture was Art Deco, although Louise Beurre, known throughout the third arrondissement of Paris as Louisa Louis, was the only woman in the entire village who would have been able to tell.

"I can see why they're looking for help, if the young mistress is reduced to answering the door."

A short while later Sarah Rosenberg entered the parlour, followed by her daughter. She moved silently like a ghost, shoulders straight, arms behind her back, forehead down. Louise straightened her dress and put on her most cheerful, confident, self-assured expression.

"Lisa tells me you are seeking a position."

"That's right, madam."

"And your references are...?"

Louise's hands turned icy cold. "My references," another sentence with no possible end, "My references..." she finally answered:

"I worked for many years in Paris."

"Paris is not an employer. In whose employ were you?"

Mother and daughter both shared the same repartee, though the mother spoke with a dryness the child had not yet developed.

"I worked as an actress. At the Théâtre de l'Ambigu-Comique, you know? No."

It may well have been a shadow of horror that passed across the pale face of Sarah Rosenberg, while Lisa stroked her yellow dog and fidgeted at her mother's side.

"And for how long did you occupy that position?"

"For two years, madam. I left the troupe after two years."

"And you returned here."

"No, madam. I remained abroad for another ten years or so."

"And what did you do during those ten years?"

Louise wasn't prepared for that. Truth be told, she wasn't prepared for anything but smiles, impressed looks, expressions of delight at her exotic accent. Her adventures overseas had placed her in a position of superiority that, she now realized, was pure fantasy.

"What did I do?"

Sarah Rosenberg's big, cold eyes focused directly on Louise's mouth. Louise attempted to recover as best she could with a lie:

"I travelled in Turkey."

"And?"

"And, well, the Turkish baths..."

"What about the Turkish baths?"

Louise felt the ground shift ever more beneath her feet.

"Forgive me, madam. I was under the impression you were seeking someone to look after your Turkish baths. But I assure you I am a very fast study, and I can adapt to any other tasks."

Sarah Rosenberg frowned at such confusion, coming on the heels, as it did, of her having, that very morning, to order the cook—who'd once again put salt in her coffee—to better label her condiments.

"I'm sorry, Miss Louis, but I'm afraid that you simply will not do. You show up here in extravagant velvet, incapable of producing the slightest reference, with an entirely incoherent explanation. It's all so muddled, whereas I prefer precision. As for the Turkish baths, I'm afraid you have been misinformed. While Spencer Wood does indeed have baths, we never use them. But no hard feelings—she softened slightly—and since the road to the village is long, our driver will take you back."

She left the parlour the same way she had entered, which is to say, virtually levitating.

On the drive back, Louise brooded in her seat as the chauffeur told madcap stories of his days as a helmsman. The first thing she saw when she walked into the widow Clot's house was the poor woman lying on the floor, in tears, her left foot jammed in the ash bucket.

6

RENÉE LEPINE watering the flowers in her window boxes—a scene as ordinary as any—except for the fact that that very morning, for the second time in a week, Old Mr. Roux went out of his way to walk over and stand in front of her, a sly expression on his face.

"Poor Louise Beurre, isn't that so!"

If it had been about any other woman, Renée would have felt entirely indifferent, but since the subject was Louise, she couldn't help but lean forward and lend a scarlet but attentive ear.

"She's looking for work! You know, when I said she'd been a flop with all that vaudeville and marionette nonsense, I thought she must have at least earned a pretty penny for her antics.

Well, I was wrong! She shows up back here as deflated as a balloon, and do you know, she can hardly even scrape together enough to pay the widow Clot for her bed and board!"

The news left Renée torn between pity and satisfaction; if Louise had been heralded home like a queen, she would have been hard to win over again, but knowing she was in trouble, Renée suddenly felt it a less impossible feat, and her thoughts turned to rescuing her.

"She even went to Spencer Wood. Can you believe it! Sarah Rosenberg treated her like a vagabond. She didn't so much as offer her a cup of tea, I hear. Oh, they are indeed seeking help at the manor, but they weren't taken in by Louise's pirouettes. They have a keen eye, those Rosenberg ladies. And proud as peacocks, into the bargain!"

Renée imagined her Louise rejected, turned away, sad and alone at the widow Clot's house. Tears sprang to her eyes, a fact that didn't escape Old Man Roux, who was already being carried off by the wind, calling out "Give my greetings to the pensioner!" as he disappeared into the distance, his coattails clinging to the backs of his legs.

7

SCRAWNY LITTLE CELESTE always cut back home through the woods. A stick-like figure herself, she was right at home in the scrubby forest. The shortcut through the woods took half the time as taking the road, which wound its way around the entire village before heading towards Spencer Wood. Once she'd crossed the forest—a stretch of trees a mile wide—she would pop out onto her own property like a gremlin, only a hundred feet or so from her house. Stitching her way back and forth through the woods every day, Celeste followed exactly the same route each time.

She rarely felt afraid. Mostly because she'd never experienced any real danger, but also because she'd never been one to fear death, which was merely The Great Rest that would follow The Great Toil. Quite the opposite of her late mother, who used to always greet her in surprise: "Oh Celeste, it's you! I thought you were dead," she would grumble as she leaned over her cooking pots, a drop hanging from the end of her nose.

After work and on belote nights, Celeste would walk through the village, cut between two houses, and make her way to the edge of the woods, where she would hitch up her skirts and jump over the ditch, her feet sinking into the clay, bulrushes whipping her thighs, then disappear between the trees into the quiet darkness. She liked hearing the water-soaked moss squelch beneath her feet, her tracks imprinted on the ground.

It was raining lightly, it was past ten o'clock, night had fallen. Ginette, still recovering from her strained back, had invited them—her and Margot—to join her, her husband, and the wretched children he had given her, for dinner.

Celeste hurried home, not because of the rain, but because she wanted to work on the knitting she'd been trying to finish for weeks. The unfinished piece was weighing on her, and now it irritated her so much she almost wished she'd never started it. She would happily have gotten up in the middle of the night to work on it, but given her sense of discipline, she would never have tolerated the thought of dozing off while she toiled. "Best to choose the lesser of two evils," she liked to say.

She was halfway home, deep in the woods, when a branch cracked nearby. "An animal," she thought, without twitching or breaking stride. Her steps were quick, her body a mere wisp, and this part of the forest wasn't the densest; when she looked up, she could even see a patch of sky and stars ringed by the dried crowns of the ash trees.

Behind her, closer this time, another crack, that she again dismissed off-hand. "An animal following me," she thought, without slowing. Then a third, fourth, fifth, sixth, seventh crack, she counted up to ten of them, irregular, heavy, accompanied by sighs and low moans. "Not an animal, after all," she thought to herself, and picked up the pace.

8

BELLA WEBB LIKED TO DAWDLE on the streets of the village and the road to Spencer Wood in the evenings, even though she lived at the far end of another road.

That rainy evening, after spotting Celeste leaving Ginette's house and heading to the woods to take God only knew what trail, she reread a letter she had received the day before from a man with whom she had been corresponding.

Two months earlier, she had decided the time had come to take another husband. She had been grieving the deaths of her Damasus and their young daughter Lucy for over a year, and she'd been working hard every day to hang onto her pride and her home.

The ad Bella had placed in the newspaper in another county was clear and to the point:

*Distinguished widow in the county of *** seeks to make the acquaintance of a respectable and well-to-do gentleman with a view to uniting fortunes and fates. Serious enquiries only, to be followed by a visit in person. Crooks and destitutes abstain.*

Her ad generated a handful of enthusiastic replies, and Bella had begun corresponding with two men, one of whom quickly proved to be an out-and-out liar, and the other, a well-off man in his fifties named Marcus.

In his last letter he had announced that he'd sold his farm and would be joining her in her county the following week, whereupon he would marry her and live and prosper by her side—a true romantic.

What a wonderful day she'd spent composing in her mind the reply she'd send him that very evening, so impatient was she to take them into her home, he and the two thousand dollars he'd promised to bring along!

Bella decided not to linger that evening. The rain had chilled her, and her pace quickened. As she crossed the village square, she stepped in a puddle and the water immediately soaked through her weathered boots. Up ahead, Celeste had already disappeared between the trees.

She walked briskly the rest of the way, stopping only once, when she thought she heard a distant cry.

Once back home, she lit the oil lamp, sat down at the table, and set about carefully composing the reply her suitor had been dreaming of.

My dear, dear friend,

I am the happiest woman in the world. I know you will come and that you will be mine for all time. Your letters have convinced me that you are the man for me. You, above all, the kindest man that could be. Think how happy we will be, just the two of us, alone. I can't imagine anything more wonderful. I think of you night and day, and the thought quickens my heart..

Dearest Marcus, I love you so. Come, and be prepared to stay forever.

Bella

9

FROM OUTSIDE THE HOUSE, you'd be forgiven for thinking he'd dozed off in his big olive-green chair. A little notebook on his lap, a pen in his left hand, eyes lowered. He was jotting down thoughts, aphorisms—mind you, he'd never have used that word—ideas that crossed his mind. That's how he spent his evenings, sitting at the window, his only occasional distraction the one-eyed cat that would come and curl up at his feet.

His infirmity had confined him to a wheelchair for so long that he no longer suffered at the thought. He perceived things through the prism of his former life, before the accident—before he turned twenty—and mornings still brought a smile to his face, days still passed in a flash, and evenings calmed him. Over the years he had come to understand that his situation, trying as it might be, provided a sense of routine that, while not necessarily enjoyable, was nonetheless bearable. Things were always the same, only they presented themselves in different ways.

When the sun was shining, he could spend the day on the porch whittling bits of wood. When it rained, he would listen to the sound of the drops on the tin roof, and feel happy to be protected from the rain.

He would have preferred it if Celeste had worked a little less. But that would have been asking a lot, would have been asking too much.

When evening fell, he would scan the edge of the woods until he spotted a movement in the leaves that signalled the return of his wife, as if a giant were cutting a wide swath through the trees, and when tiny Celeste would emerge, her skirts hiked up, he would smile at her determined step and her brusque gestures. She always looked as if she were heading up a marching band.

Basil put away his notebook at ten o'clock and waited, his gaze fixed on the strip of trees at the far end of the property. The moon shone brightly on the tall grass that separated the candlelit pane of his window from the darkened woods.

A few trees tremored, then fluttered, the canes of an elderberry bush parted, and Celeste rushed out, tripping over a root and galloping towards the door with nary a wave or a glance at the man who was watching her. Slamming the door behind her, she burst into the house with a terrified cry:

"Oh, Basil!"

Her husband froze in his armchair.

"My dear Celeste, what on earth is the matter?"

Struggling to find the words, she extinguished the lamp, crouched beside the window, her chin resting on the sill, huffing like a whale. Basil stroked her hair:

"Won't you tell me what happened?"

"Be quiet and look!"

He squinted at the row of shrubs edging the forest, not knowing what he was looking for. Celeste had excellent eyesight, and she saw it first, and whispered:

"Look! There!"

Basil leaned closer to the window. From the same gap in the woods where Celeste had popped out, a silhouette slowly appeared, struggling and limping as it headed straight for the house, for the dark window where two sets of shining eyes stared intently at it.

"Who is it?"

Celeste shook her head.

The shadow advanced with a heavy step. They could see now: a woman, a tall, thin woman.

When she got to within six feet of the house, she stopped, the blackness still masking her face, then her gaze turned to them in the window, or at least, they thought that's where she was looking, but could she see them? Celeste, her chin still resting on the windowsill, held her breath as Basil, paralyzed by fear, crushed her shoulders in his grip.

The woman turned her head, and Basil started and Celeste blinked as her profile revealed itself to them. That long nose, that chin: Renée Lepine.

"What's she doing?"

Renée turned again, backed up a few steps, looked again towards the window and, for a split second, the whiteness of the moon illuminated her, her unbuttoned dress, her bootlaces trailing, her foggy eyes open yet closed at the same time. She turned back and disappeared into the forest.

Basil trembled.

"What was she doing?"

Celeste, still sitting cross-legged on the floor, redid her hair in a bun and mumbled through a mouthful of hairpins:

"Nothing. She was sleeping."

10

AT TEN O'CLOCK, Renée opened her eyes and sat up in bed without glancing at the clock. The pensioner must have managed to make his own breakfast, although the thought barely crossed the servant's mind. Upon waking she had been struck by a furtive idea she wanted to put into action before she changed her mind.

Many years before, she had worked in a neighbouring town for six months for Madam de Sainte-Colombe, a vague acquaintance of Marquette the pensioner. She was an elderly woman, somewhat crippled and with no money to her name. The pensioner had lent Renée to her for a while, to help her out. Perhaps the woman could take on Louise Beurre; that would bring her closer to

Renée. It would be better than with those village store busybodies, it was better than the disgusting pensioner, it was better than nothing. It might not be a match for Spencer Wood, but it was certainly better than nothing. And if it meant earning Louise's gratitude, then it was worth a try.

As she left her room, she noticed the back door banging in the wind. There was nothing she found more annoying.

She thought about taking the train straight away to visit Madam de Sainte-Colombe, then she reconsidered. The woman must have been nearly seventy back when she used to be her employer, which meant she'd be almost eighty. If she was still alive.

"Will she be at home today? Is she still alive?"

There was no way of knowing without calling ahead, but a woman of such humble means surely didn't have a telephone. If she was even still alive.

When Renée stepped off the train, she was suddenly struck with a violent cramp, and she had to sit down on the platform, clutching her stomach with both hands. A few passersby stared at her, wide-eyed. A rosy-cheeked man piped up:

"Miss?"

She waved him away.

"Just something I ate on the train. It'll pass."

The man walked off, and ten minutes later, she got to her feet, her forehead slick with sweat. It was the first time she'd ever experienced such a malaise.

Madam de Sainte-Colombe had lived above a bookstore. Renée remembered it well: a vast, empty, dark, quiet place.

She climbed the metal staircase and knocked three times on the door. A spider brushed past her ear. She let out a little cry and knocked again, harder this time. In the end she hammered on the door, calling "Hellooo! Hellooo!" while the spider spun its thread across the door, creeping dangerously close to her hand.

"Sainte-Colombe, Sainte-Colombe..."

The bookstore owner frowned as he repeated the name like an incantation. Alerted by the banging on the door to the upstairs apartment, he'd come out to ask what Renée wanted. She'd gone into his store, where she peppered the man with questions as she leaned over the counter like a beggarwoman.

"You mean the elderly woman who used to live upstairs and spent her days reading? She would devour every book before we could even put in on the shelves."

"Yes, that's her. You're right: She would stay in and read all the time. I used to come down here to pick up new books for her. Do you remember me?"

"Hmmm, maybe... Yes, now I think I do."

He seemed content to leave it at that, and he went back to his book with a satisfied look on his face.

"So, do you know what became of her?"

The man looked up in irritation:

"No, I have no idea."

"Did she pass away? Is she still alive?"

"How on earth would I know?"

Renée refused to give up.

"Surely you recall the day she moved out."

"That must have been over a year ago. It's been empty ever since. So, what of it?"

"Well, did she leave in a hearse?"

The storekeeper pursed his lips at the insolence of the pale-faced woman.

"No, I do not recall any hearse. Or any floral wreaths or funeral procession or priests or mourners, for that matter. What more can I say?"

"Well, where would an ailing woman in this town go to end her days?"

Sainte-Colombe Hospital.

"Surely not," Renée thought to herself.

And yet.

The nun at the front door led her to a large, stuffy, dank dormitory. It smelled of lead and greasy hair.

"Madam de Sainte-Colombe. The bed beside the window."

Renée walked across the room, her arms crossed over her chest. On either side—she could barely bring herself to look—white-haired heads poked out from beneath the sheets. Scrawny bodies, all alike, some several to a bed, moaning. Sinister music playing uninterrupted.

At the far end, a bed with three heads. Renée stopped. On the left, a huge woman lay snoring, her body swollen all over, her cheeks and neck sprouting long white hairs. On the right, a tiny woman curled in a ball, her gaze distant, almost girl-like, but with a gaping mouth, her breath coming in volcanic bursts.

And in the middle, Madam de Sainte-Colombe. Cheeks wizened, bones jutting, eyes wide and glassy, hair unkempt. Waiting to die on a mattress squeezed between two strangers.

Renée tried her best to compose her face in a cheerful expression, but the bedridden residents, at least those who still had their eyesight, were used to the graveness etched in the faces of those gazing at them from the foot of their beds.

"Madam de Sainte-Colombe?"

The woman in the middle looked at her, but only because Renée happened to be within her field of vision. There didn't appear to be the slightest flicker of life left in those empty eyes, so far as she could tell.

"It's Renée Lepine."

The tiny shell of a woman on the right turned her head and shoulders towards the voice. Her mouth still hanging open, her absent gaze fell on Renée as she sunk further between the springs of the mattress.

"Madam de Sainte-Colombe. I've come to see you. It's Renée Lepine."

The woman with the whiskered chin woke and licked her lips. There were now three sets of eyes staring at the visitor. She examined each one. There might still have been a shred of sense in the big hirsute one. Renée turned to her and smiled. In return she was met with a series of blinks, an irregular string of blinks not unlike Morse code. Her eyelids appeared to be closing, but never actually touched. Renée found the effect disturbing and dizzying.

She pictured herself fifteen years older, emaciated, dishevelled, forgotten in that same bed between two unclean strangers. Feeling their feet brush against her when they moved. Hearing their throats clear. Recognizing their coughs and their odours. A three-headed monster.

"What's the point? There's nothing to be learned from these women."

But her desire to help Louise was stronger than ever. She stopped to talk to the nun again on her way out:

"I'm a friend. She doesn't speak anymore, does she?"

"Madam de Sainte-Colombe has her good days. But if you ask me, no, I don't think she'll ever speak again."

"Please write to me if anything changes."

As she stepped out onto the road, she was seized by another cramp that left her doubled over in pain.

11

IN THE BIG, CLEAN, dark apartment above the bookstore, Madam de Sainte-Colombe would spend her days reading books. In her parlour, a large bookcase held them by the ton; books about history, for the most part. Ten years later, on a lumpy mattress in a hospital that bore the same name as hers, it was as if she had forgotten the very existence of those tomes that had almost entirely occupied her life.

In forty years of widowhood, her life had eventually become set like tracks in the snow. She lived methodically, settling into her chair in the large living room later in the morning, around nine o'clock. On the coffee table, several gigantic volumes of an encyclopedia would lie open. Madam de Sainte-Colombe would read one page a day, taking notes all the while in a black notebook. She would reread her notes several times, crossing out words here and there—who knew which ones?—before locking the notebook away in a drawer of the dresser.

Then she would dive back into the book she'd started the day before or, if she'd finished it already, the next book on her list. The list included every book on her shelves, and she would update it every week. Madam de Sainte-Colombe abhorred the sight of an empty spot on her shelves, and her servant would be sent downstairs to the bookstore as soon as her mistress finished a book, to return it and choose a new one. The bookstore owner, perfectly content with that never-ending windfall of books to sell—and resell—would take back the book, always in immaculate condition, and lend her another for a small fee. And so, the widow, in the space of thirty years, had devoured more pages than most of the men of her time.

As Madam de Sainte-Colombe soon discovered, that monkish occupation helped make solitude and reclusion much more palatable. The daily arrival of new books kept her busy and seemed to slow the passage of time. So long as there were words to be read, there would be time to read them. It was an arithmetic certainty for the old woman: her books served to crystallize time. And she would read till the very last page of even the worst, the most boring books, because they were like hiccups in her routine, moments she would recall one week, one month later: "Oh yes, that book, it nearly put me to sleep," and that monologue confirmed her very existence. She couldn't discuss the books she read with the woman who lived with her, because she had to give them back as soon as she finished them. In any case, over the years, her servants had never shown the slightest interest in their mistress's pastime.

Except Renée. During the months she lived with Madam de Sainte-Colombe, she learned to accept—first with amazement, then with boredom, and finally, with tenderness—the slow pace that marked time in that silent home. The apartment was, in a way, an extension of the bookstore: its inventory stretching to the floor above, where the turnover was sometimes greater than that of the store itself.

Renée was a curious, voracious woman, and it pained her to see passing through her hands so many books she would never have the luxury of reading until, one day, Madam de Sainte-

Colombe, who must have sensed her suffering, whispered these words in a magnanimous gesture as she handed her a book, her lips, as usual, barely parting as she spoke:

"Keep it for a day or two. Read it, if you like."

Taken aback, Renée thanked her and took the book to her room, glancing at the title as she went: *The Science of Dreams.* Although disappointed—she preferred novels—she was intrigued, and devoured the book in next to no time. The author, who was a follower of the great scientists and philosophers, dissected dreams and their mechanisms in an extraordinary prose, a style that was a little too florid for Renée, but that the spiritual Madam de Sainte-Colombe found very much to her liking.

One chapter dealt with nightmares, another with sleepwalking, still others with premonitions and trances, the texts accompanied by expressionist drawings depicting clawed feet and shadows, and then a series of short legends: *The Horse of Death, The Dancing Phantom, Spiders of the Night...* Renée found the drawings repulsive, and couldn't see what they could possibly teach about the science of dreams.

She finished the book on the second evening, and since it was too late to drop by the bookstore, she left it on her bedside table. The final chapter was all about alleged cases of fatal dreams, whose intensity or outcome invariably resulted in the death of the dreamer. Renée was skeptical, but the author's cold and lugubrious descriptions made an impression on her nonetheless, especially the one about the woman who became paralyzed in her own nightmare and perished, immobile in her bed, asphyxiated, her eyes wide open, crushed by some indescribable force.

"What nonsense! If the nights were filled with horses, phantoms, and spiders, as the book says, they'd make such a racket that sleep would be impossible."

Lying face down, the servant blew out the candle and pulled the sheets up tight around her neck, a gesture she might have attributed to a passing draft, but that was more likely connected to her recent reading material. Unmoving and uncomfortable, she would have liked to turn over onto her back, but no, she didn't. She strained her ears, listening for the slightest cracking in the walls, holding her breath all the better to hear, and the more she paid attention to the night surrounding her, the more she figured the night was paying attention to her, the more the slightest rustling of sheets would unleash pandemonium.

It was past midnight before Renée finally relaxed her back and arms, letting the blanket she'd been gripping tight for hours slide down onto her shoulders, closing her eyes, and forgetting about her need to listen for any imperfections in the silence.

It was also at that very moment that silence chose to embrace perfection. As Renée slept, the darkness, disturbed by not a single sliver of moonlight, enveloped the entire room and, indeed, it seemed in that rare instant that the slightest noise would have created an infernal din and upset the natural order of things.

But the slightest noise did come. From the other side of the closed door, the sound of slippers shuffling across the floor. And on the wooden door panel, there came a dry, resounding knock.

Renée sat up ramrod straight in bed, quickly pulling the covers up over her shoulders to form a little pyramid, and she held her breath, eyes immobile (since there was nothing to see), her back bare (something she couldn't abide), her back damp and vulnerable.

"Stop breathing."

That won't be enough.

"Stop your heart from beating."

The shuffling receded down the hall, then came back, went away again, came back again. Lungs emptied, heart stopped, Renée knew it was only Madam de Sainte-Colombe on the other side of the door, but she couldn't help those chapters from *The Science of Dreams* from racing through her mind, especially the images she'd found most ridiculous, especially the one of "The Dancing Phantom," whose billowing skirts reminded her of the flounces on her mistress's nightdress.

"Old Sainte-Colombe is no ghost."

Those absurd words did little to reassure her. Her bosom rose and fell, her heart raced, she was struck by a nasty cramp. If she'd been standing, her legs would surely have given out.

An eternity passed, but the widow continued to pace back and forth, but the sun refused to rise, but Renée still didn't move a muscle.

Finally, she shifted a foot, pushed back the bedcovers, and climbed out of bed. She waited until the woman had passed her door before cracking it open an inch and hazarding a glance out into the hallway.

Madam de Sainte-Colombe was pacing the hall, her arms swinging, her long white braid hanging down her back. The outline of her scrawny thighs showed through her threadbare cotton nightgown, a fleeting draft bringing goosebumps to her arms as she passed by the parlour.

Renée recalled a passage from *The Science of Dreams.*

The sleepwalker must on no account be disturbed. If he or she commits any grotesque or deplorable acts, let them be. A sudden awakening will only unleash their madness by prompting a collision between the world of dreams and the world of the living.

She thought it a bit much to contrast dreams and life. But, nevertheless, the words sent a chill down her spine.

The widow was still dragging her bony body back and forth, her knees cracking with each step. When she got to the end of the hall, she would turn, walk back towards her room, turn back again, and start all over again, again three times, again one hundred times. How pale and ghost-like she looked from behind, cast against the inky darkness of the apartment!

"Madam de Sainte-Colombe?"

Renée grunted more than spoke the words. The old woman reached the wall, turned around, and walked past her servant with not a sound.

"Madam de Sainte-Colombe. Madam, go back to bed."

Up and down the hallway, the braid swung back and forth in time to the sleepwalker's steps. Renée began to feel exasperated. More annoyed than frightened, she was ready to go back to bed, but her door didn't lock, and she feared Madam de Sainte-Colombe might veer off course and end up in her room, where she would give her a dreadful scare.

While Renée hovered in her doorway, her mistress stopped in her tracks and headed instead to the kitchen, where she could be heard rustling in the cupboards, the sound of glasses clinking, then she came back out and walked into the parlour, a match in hand. Suddenly there was a scratching sound, and the books caught fire immediately, the shelves ignited, the walls turned crimson, the house ablaze.

12

FOR MARCUS PILGRIM to flee the nest and head off down the dirt road upon which he'd taken his very first steps, without so much as a glance back, there had to be a good reason. A creature of habit, having acquired a thousand and one of them since his early childhood, he, like his father, his grandfather, and his great-grandfather before him, ran the family farm, one of the most prosperous in the county.

When his mother was still alive, she used to say that a storm of the heart could uproot an entire forest. Marcus, ever pragmatic, listened to her words, imagining torrents and squalls tearing great oak trees right out of the ground.

But today it was neither wind nor water that was carrying him far from his home; it was the elegantly penned letters of the widow Bella Webb.

At the other end of that same dirt road, some sixty miles away, Bella could hardly contain her excitement. A man, another pair of arms, a presence, and two thousand dollars. While she waited, she bleached, scrubbed, polished, waxed, dusted, scoured, scraped, purged, and deterged.

When, in the early hours of a warm evening, the cart pulled by two strong mares turned the corner and appeared in front of the house, Bella tucked a wisp of hair back into her bun, wiped her callused hands on her apron, and went out onto the porch, where she set her left foot one step down from her right, her hand on the post, a smile on her face, the very picture of hope and anticipation.

Marcus had been running over and over in his mind for the past few hours the wonderful promise his far-off sweetheart had made to him in writing:

Dearest Marcus, I love you so. Come, and be prepared to stay forever.

13

A LETTER FOR RENÉE, the first in five years. The pensioner Marquette's eyes crossed inquisitively as he handed it to her: *Sainte-Colombe Hospital,* it said, in the corner of the envelope.

"That's where Madam de Sainte-Colombe lives."

The pensioner's eyes uncrossed.

"Have you been to see her? How is Diane, the poor dear?"

He wasn't particularly interested. Renée noticed his hands wandering restlessly across the folds of his shirt.

"Not well at all, I am afraid. She's bedridden, she didn't recognize me, she doesn't speak at all."

Renée tore open the envelope and read the contents aloud, since she sensed from the pensioner's presence that this was what he expected:

Dear Miss Lepage (it's *Lepine*, Renée sighed),

I am writing to regretfully inform you that Madam Diane de Sainte-Colombe, who was in increasingly poor health in recent days, went to meet her maker yesterday morning. As her sole visitor since she was admitted to the hospital, you are welcome, should you so desire, to come and collect her few belongings. We know of no family members.

Sister Mary Felicity

The pensioner mumbled a few words of sympathy and disappeared off into his office, although not before reminding Renée to scrub the parquet.

She poured her disappointment into the wooden floorboards. Her last hope of finding a position for Louise had been extinguished along with Madam de Sainte-Colombe—not that, in her state, immobile in a hospital bed, she would have been looking to hire a servant—but Renée had allowed herself to imagine a miraculous recovery, bordering on a resurrection. Her plan, which had sparked in her such excitement only a week before, now seemed impossibly distant, like a dream that fades away, like a drawing with no outline, a drawing that's nothing but smudges.

The dead woman's belongings were of little interest to her, since she knew she'd been poor and very prim: they surely consisted of nothing more than religious objects and silk handkerchiefs, perhaps a last sentimental trinket. But Renée Lepine understood, at least in part, the reclusive and austere life Diane de Sainte-Colombe had led; it was up to her to collect what remained of a woman whom everyone had forgotten, to go back to that town, and back to that bed in the middle of which a gap now appeared, between the big bearded lady and the emaciated little one. In her pessimistic mind, the thought even occurred to her that the gap was now waiting for her, that it would swallow her up the way it had swallowed up Madam de Sainte-Colombe, a gap that gobbled up lonely women and spat them back out into a dark lake.

So lost was she in her melancholy meanderings that she didn't notice a spider venturing closer to a puddle that had formed on the freshly scrubbed floor. Each of its eight legs came to a halt, and there it stayed for a moment as the servant continued her cleaning. By the time she went to wipe up the water, the nasty little creature had disappeared.

With her bad leg, Renée had trouble getting back to her feet. When the doorbell rang, it took her a lifetime to struggle upright. Needless to say, the pensioner Marquette didn't move a muscle and stayed glued to his chair like a gargoyle to its gutter.

Celeste didn't wait for someone to answer the door and strode straight in, as vigorously as ever, her heels clickety-clacking across the parquet floor.

"Should you really be scrubbing the floor like that, what with your leg, Renée?"

If the pensioner sitting just the other side of the partly opened door heard her remark, he didn't react.

"I don't really have a choice, Celeste."

"Go on, now. You take a rest and let me finish up. It's just plain silly."

Since Renée knew how much Celeste enjoyed all manner of household chores, and since she couldn't abide them herself, she went into her bedroom and sat down on the bed.

"Tell me, dear."

Celeste really was putting her heart into it, scrubbing energetically, the tip of her tongue sticking out.

"Tell me, how are you?"

The little slip of a woman had to raise her voice in order for Renée to hear her from the next room. Renée wasn't sure she liked the direction this conversation was taking, but since she so rarely talked, she made an effort to sound affable.

"I'm fine, I'm fine. And you?"

"Fine."

"And Basil?"

"Oh, he's the same as ever. Still confined to his chair, but never a complaint from the dear man."

Renée smiled. She liked Basil. He was a quiet man, and he managed to do all kinds of little jobs, even though he couldn't get around.

"How about your sleep?"

Something caught in Celeste's voice as she said the word. Renée, who never missed a beat, picked up on it right away.

"My sleep? What of it?"

The brush strokes on the wooden floor slowed.

"I mean: Do you sleep well?"

What a curious question.

"Very well, my dear. And you?"

"Like a log. Like a baby. Basil, too. Restful, dreamless nights."

Renée was amused by the strange turn the conversation was taking.

"Same for me, Celeste. I never dream."

A silence settled over them for a few minutes, the only sounds being the brush rasping against the floor and the pensioner Marquette clearing his throat in his office. Celeste didn't seem to know what else to say, and the conversation drifted towards the weather, the rain, and big Bella. The pensioner's ears perked up.

"Have you heard Bella is getting married? To a rich widower from another county. She placed an ad, you know?"

Renée thought the whole thing utterly ridiculous, but what else would you expect from Bella?

"No, that's news to me, Celeste. But after all, she's been on her own in that house for a year now. It's probably a good thing."

"Still, a man she's never even met..."

Renée fixed her hair as she sat before her mottled mirror.

"You know, Celeste, if there's anyone who's to be pitied, it's that poor fool who doesn't know what he's letting himself in for."

On the other side of the door, the pensioner Marquette blushed.

Once the floor was done, Renée promptly sent Celeste on her way with a thank-you:

"You'd better be off. I wouldn't put it past the pensioner to ask you to do the walls and ceilings too, while you're at it. I always refuse, on account I don't have a head for heights."

14

IT HAD BEEN FIVE DAYS since he'd moved in with her.

Bella and her Marcus. They'd gone to the bank the very first day, to deposit the two thousand dollars.

On the second day, she'd shown him the house, the land, all the jobs that needed doing, the store where she worked, she'd introduced him to Celeste, to her boss Margot, to Ginette, to a few other acquaintances, she'd taken him to the village and into the forest, and he hadn't had much to say. He was terribly quiet.

She had reread their correspondence, those letters that flowed and sang so sweetly, the story they had created for themselves with words like *mine, time, love, above*. And she lifted her gaze and saw Marcus outside, stacking firewood. Marcus, so small, so quiet; and she, Bella, so big, so strong.

On the third night he crept into her bedroom like a mouse into the pantry. The footsteps of a child as he approached her bed, laid his soft hands on her, and he trembled, he was clammy and cold. She nearly cried in despair.

From time to time he looked up at the window where she was sewing. The smile he gave her turned her stomach to acid. There was nothing to smile about when their movements were so completely at odds. They spoke not the same language, they were hopelessly mismatched, with their awkward embraces.

She'd confided in Margot, but her boss waved away her anger with a glib remark that Bella had refused with a shake of her head; no, it wasn't a matter of giving themselves time, of getting to know each other, of accepting one another. It all came down to their deeply opposing natures.

Marcus came in when it got dark and sat down at the table. Bella had prepared a meal of headcheese, and they ate in heavy silence. She watched him handle his knife and fork, she dissected his every movement and found fault with each and every one. He was too careful. He set his cutlery down too meticulously. He drank in too-small sips. He sat up too straight.

When he felt that pair of eyes examining him, Marcus placed his hands flat on the table and gave Bella a broad smile. In the flickering light of the oil lamp, deep furrows appeared on either side of the man's mouth and across his brow.

When his companion failed to return his kindness, he turned back to his meal, but as he did, he dropped his fork under the table, and struggled terribly to bend over and stretch out his arm to pick it up. He banged his head on the edge of the table as he came out from beneath, and when he took his seat again his face was flushed.

His red cheeks and the lines on his skin remained imprinted in Bella's mind, and she saw him, once and for all, for what he was: small, clumsy, old, weak.

15

Seeking honest and hard-working maid-in-waiting. Experience required. Please contact Madam Rosenberg at Spencer Wood.

Renée felt a pang as she read the ad. It was the position for which her Louise had been turned down.

All evening long she imagined the type of women who would go knocking at the manor door. Prim little women in freshly pressed dresses, their voices hushed, their eyes expressionless. There were scant few of those types around these parts. They would no doubt come from the city, where she'd heard work was becoming scarcer. They wouldn't have ever heard of Spencer Wood. They'd be good at hairstyling, coordinating, smoothing, buttoning, attending, unbuckling, darning, and putting away.

Another would take up the position, the mistress would appear in the village, well dressed and content, and would pass by Louise without paying her the slightest notice.

Renée fell asleep late that night, as she often did, worn out by her memories and her melancholy. Long after the pensioner had gone to bed, she finally felt herself fall.

She was shivering in the bottom of a shiny white tub, a huge tub with enamelled sides. She lay curled in a ball, naked, in five inches of water. The sides of the tub rose so high that all she could see above was the dark, starless sky.

She could hear the voice of big Bella somewhere in the distance.

Water started to flow into the tub, all over her trembling body. Hot water, first a trickle, then a gush, then finally a torrent, and the water was filling her ears, but she could still hear a cackling and she knew it was Bella, talking and laughing.

And she opened her eyes; she was lying on her back. All she could see was the dusty old chandelier hanging from the ceiling, its candle cups yellowed, its arms twisted, and in one of the cups, a close-up reflection of herself, of her bed from which emerged her grey head, her eyes bulging, mouth wide open and ready to talk, or rather to scream, to drag her out of her suffocating, petrifying dream.

16

"I WENT TO MARQUETTE'S place yesterday."

Celeste was sweeping the kitchen floor with brisk strokes of her broom. Basil, sitting at the window, his notebook on his lap, smiled as he listened to her.

"Uh-huh?"

She was attacking an overlooked corner of the room where a spider had managed to weave a few strands of its web.

"Since she stopped coming to the store, I never bump into her anymore. So I thought I'd drop in and see her. And while I was there, I gave her a hand with her chores. Can you believe it, the pensioner has her scrubbing the floors on all fours! With her leg and all!"

"Hmm."

"It's too much for her. You should see her struggling to stand up. It's not right!"

Basil jotted a few words in his notebook.

"Just as well I went to see her. I asked how she was sleeping, too."

Her husband looked up.

"How she was *sleeping*?"

She stopped a moment to tuck a few wisps of hair back into her bun, which was always coming undone.

"I asked her if she slept well. Of course, I didn't mention the other night. She surely has no recollection of it. I imagine when you wake up, you don't usually remember. Or else, you just think you dreamed it. Even though her eyes were open."

"Anyway, it's not as though we can do anything about it."

Celeste stopped sweeping for an instant.

"No, that's true."

Basil gave her his usual look, one of satisfaction and contentment.

"It's true, but still, it would be a shame if something were to happen to her. If she sleepwalks so far from home, just imagine what could happen."

"I'd rather not, my dear."

She sighed.

"Well, I'd rather not either, but that doesn't stop me from worrying about her. Renée is all alone, after all. And don't think for a minute the pensioner is going to look after her. She doesn't have her Celeste, you know."

He leaned back happily in his olive-coloured chair.

"It's none of our business, dear Celeste. It's no one's business."

She closed her eyes.

"Right you are, dear Basil."

17

*Distinguished widow in the county of *** seeks to make the acquaintance of a respectable and well-to-do gentleman with a view to uniting fortunes and fates. Serious enquiries only, to be followed by a visit in person. Crooks and destitutes abstain.*

This time, Bella Webb placed her ad in the weekly of a far-off county to the north.

18

AS SHE SAT IN THE TRAIN on her way to the city, Renée tried to focus her gaze. A huge field stretched away to her left, in the middle of which stood a fir tree with an impenetrable tangle of branches, and she trained her eyes on it until she could see it no longer.

At the Sainte-Colombe Hospital, the nun who greeted her wasn't the same one as the time before, the one who had written to her. When Renée enquired after her, the nun standing before her, face as wrinkled as an accordion, handed her a tin box.

"Sister Mary Felicity went to meet her maker yesterday, dear."

The visitor shook her head in disbelief.

"But she seemed so young!"

"Oh, she was over fifty, you know."

Renée opened the box glumly, glancing distractedly inside. She pictured in her mind the nun who had greeted her a few weeks earlier.

"Was she ill?"

The nun leaned closer and grasped her by the wrist.

"Boiled to death, she was. Fell into a vat of hot water."

She stepped back and pursed her lips, her head bobbing gently up and down. A minute passed in silence, the only sound a few rasping coughs escaping from the dank dormitory.

The nun pointed to the box.

"Madam de Sainte-Colombe's things. She passed away in her sleep, you know."

Renée thanked her. She wanted to see once more the skinny little woman and the fat whiskered one, the final companions of the late Madam de Sainte-Colombe, who had already been replaced by another old biddy, an enormous woman, her skin as smooth as a slug's, eyes red, cheeks chapped from crying. This one was a talker.

"Madam, madam, madam, madam, madam, madam, madam, madam."

The woman's gaze and her never-ending recitation followed Renée's every movement, causing her to twitch violently. Sainte-Colombe, dead in her bed for hours before anyone noticed, no doubt. Jammed between two strangers who, that night, had slept with a cadaver.

Renée didn't look at the deceased woman's possessions until she was sitting in the train. Rosary beads, a handkerchief, a vial with no label, a pearl necklace, and *The Science of Dreams*.

19

THE REPLIES TO BELLA'S ad weren't so quick to come this time. In the austere northern county, people were more wary, it seems, of hearts that were up for grabs.

The widow went back to her routine and to her work at the store, and while it pained her, she thought she was nonetheless better off there than by the side of a man who inspired evil thoughts in her. One pleasant afternoon, she toiled for hours splitting wood, the thwack of her axe echoing for miles around, every chunk that cleaved from the trunk causing her to breathe a heavy sigh that, as the day wore on, grew into a moan, then a bellow.

She didn't stop until dusk, exhausted and unsteady on her feet, her shoulders shuddering in spasms.

That evening, she sat next to the lamp and read a book that Margot had loaned her: *The Sordid Chronicles,* two hundred pages recounting in gruesome detail—gleaned allegedly from the victims' families—the most macabre murders, abductions, and disappearances of the past twenty years. How much was fact and how much fiction, Bella didn't stop to wonder, enraptured as she was by the details and descriptions the author provided with such morbid enthusiasm.

Her favourite stories in the book were the most ghoulish. One featured a family, including two children, that ran a roadside inn and clobbered guests to death in their sleep, throwing the bodies into a hole they'd dug in their cellar.

The story captured Bella's attention. She imagined herself running such an inn, where people would enter through a thick embossed wood door, the floor would be varnished, there'd be a fireplace in one corner with three wing chairs before it, a handful of tables and benches where patrons could eat and drink, a four-armed chandelier, herself in the kitchen, a husband manning the bar, children who would serve and clear the tables, and satiated, happy, tired, sleepy, well-off travellers.

The next day, a letter was waiting for her, the first—highly detailed—reply to her ad:

Dear Madam,

I am a widower and own 100 acres of cleared land, some sixty cows and as many pigs, a chicken coop that's the envy of every farmer in the land, three rabbit hutches, several mighty plow horses the likes of which you will find nowhere else in the county, a maple grove with 20,000 tapped trees, as well as scores of sheep, hunting hounds, turkeys, and goats.

I have also the furniture and buildings to go with it all, as my four children are grown and gone, and my Rosie passed away two years ago.

Bella's heart beat faster as she read through the list. She tried to estimate the worth of such assets, counting on her fat fingers, and even getting up to fetch paper and pencil. No other landowner in the county possessed even a quarter of this gentleman's possessions; she could scarcely believe it.

Her joy dissipated as she read the rest of the letter.

I am seeking a pleasant and agreeable widow who shall come settle here on my land, help me with the chores, and share my life in my county.

If you would be so kind as to reply, I shall tell you more about my land and my corner of the country.

Raymond Chance

She had clearly stated in her notice—had she not?—that she sought a widower who would come live on her land, in her county, in her corner of the country, to unite their fortunes and destinies. Exile was not what she had in mind: "It is the man who must come to the woman, not the other way around," she thought to herself, furious and chagrined.

She refrained from writing back to him that evening, as her reply would surely have oozed with acrimony and desperation.

Lying in bed, she didn't fall asleep until much later. She'd been clenching her fists for hours, fretting over the sum she could have deposited at the bank—no doubt it would have been far more than Marcus Pilgrim's two thousand dollars—and the comfort it would have brought her.

20

YOUNG LUCY WEBB, while she was still alive, was better off than most of the other children in the county. A month before her disappearance, the child was skipping around the house while her parents toiled beneath a monstrous sun. Her father Damasus, a rugged, muscle-bound hulk of a man, didn't mind her galloping around and kicking up dust, but big Bella grabbed the girl by the arm as soon as she skipped within reach and shook her like an apple tree, causing her to cry out in anger. As combative as her mother, the youngster struggled free and pranced off again.

"Your daughter has no respect, husband."

"She's your daughter, too, wife."

"You're too easy on her. When I try to make her behave, you let her get away with murder as soon as my back is turned."

Her complaints tended to fall on deaf ears, as Damasus wasn't a confrontational man. He'd changed since they'd married: he held his tongue, worked harder, played cards less often, kept to himself, and avoided discussion.

That evening in the parlour, Damasus sat snoring in his chair while Bella darned socks. Lucy had found in a cupboard a small, shiny metal pistol on a wooden stand. She grabbed it by the grip and pointed it at her mother's head.

"Bang, bang," she whispered.

Her chubby little fingers searched for the trigger and, with her index nestled against its smooth curve, she slowly pressed, her eyes fixed on Bella, a dry click that was lost in the crackle of the logs crackling in the woodstove, and a spark flashed from the muzzle of her toy gun.

Lucy pressed again and again, "bang, bang," until Bella heard her and turned, staring at the child with her grubby face and gap-toothed mouth and at the pistol pointed straight at her. They stayed that way for a long while, mother and daughter, "bang, bang," and it was impossible to know what Bella Webb was thinking behind those big black eyes of hers. She dropped her darning, stood, and floated over to Lucy. Beneath her long brown skirt, her feet never seemed to leave the ground; she always walked in short strides, but her arms swung, her shoulders undulating like a bear's. When she reached her daughter's side, she stood straight as a tower, her shadow swallowing everything in her path. From a child's perspective, Bella was like a giant, and she was truly enormous.

"Don't ever touch that again."

She grabbed the gun lighter and put it away in the cupboard, without hiding it or locking it up. She didn't even close the cupboard door. She looked straight into Lucy's eyes for the longest time.

"Your daughter has no respect."

Of course, Damasus was fast asleep and didn't hear a word. She went on talking to him, staring at their daughter all the while.

"Bad things happen to young girls who are disrespectful."

Lucy fingered her mother's skirt, and Bella slapped her hand away.

"Isn't that so, husband?"

Then she went back to her chair, sat down, and picked up her darning, looking at her daughter for several long minutes, although truth be told she was looking at the wall behind Lucy, mere inches above her head.

21

AFTER THREE WEEKS OF COHABITATION, Louise Beurre and Eva Clot fell into the routine of a couple of spinsters, which suited the widow perfectly well, but which was not at all Louise's habit. Ever since the foot-in-bucket episode, the widow limped and refused to see a doctor. Perched on her stool, she would order her tenant around, telling her what to do in the house—and how to do it, too—but Louise Beurre, known in other circles as Louisa Louis, was no dummy: "If I'm going to do all this work for you, I won't be paying rent anymore."

Old Mr. Roux would drop by often, either to observe and spy on them or to tell them who he'd spied on and what he'd observed.

"Renée Lepine gets all emotional every time your name comes up, Louise."

The plates clattered in Louise Beurre's hands.

"Quiet now! Eva Clot is just next door!"

"Eva Clot, Bella Webb, Celeste, and everyone else, too... Come on, Louise Beurre, the whole village remembers. Thirteen years isn't a lifetime, even at your age."

"It's Louisa Louis now, and there's nothing to remember! If you knew everything I've been through, you would see that those thirteen years were indeed a lifetime. You're going to make me wish I never came back, you and your nasty remarks."

He simply shrugged and stared hard at her:

"Well, as it happens, I don't know everything. What is there to know? Why did you come back?"

She wasn't naive enough to entrust her secrets to that old gossipmonger, and she wasn't in the mood to tell fibs; all she really wanted was for him to leave.

"One thing's for sure—Renée Lepine certainly went out of her way to help you."

You had to hand it to Old Roux: he could pique your curiosity as quickly as others could draw their weapon, and with Renée Lepine it worked, but Louise was made of stronger stuff, and she ignored his remark.

"Give my greetings to the widow Clot," he called, on his way out.

Louise put the rest of the plates away in the cupboard, noisily and with a certain degree of discontent, as if to convey her emotion to the four plaster walls around her and to the widow napping in the next room.

22

FOR TWO DAYS, *The Science of Dreams* had been splayed out like a dead body on Renée Lepine's bedside table. She was convinced the book wanted something from her, and chided herself for thinking so. The words stayed with her, as did the impressionistic illustrations of spiders as big as basins, of shadowy figures in the fog, of black fingernails. The mere thought of lifting the dog-eared cover and catching a glimpse of one of those sentences horrified her: "Why in the devil's name had Madam de Sainte-Colombe hung on to that book?"

The pearl necklace, handkerchief, and rosary were promptly relegated to the back of Renée's drawer. As for the mysterious vial, she sniffed its contents three times a day, trying to identify the liquid. “Holy water? Too strong. Perfume? Too pungent. Poison?” She even went so far as to dip her index finger in it and lick it. “Syrup of ipecac?” There had to be something eating away at her to focus so single-mindedly on such an insignificant little bottle, so much so that it distracted her from flipping through *The Science of Dreams*, between whose pages Madam de Sainte-Colombe could well have slipped her last will and testament, some secret correspondence, or even a stash of banknotes.

The next day she watered her pansies in the window box again, perhaps hoping that Old Mr. Roux would pop by with some exciting piece of news, but the only thing she saw was a long automobile pulling out into the road and gliding beneath her window. When it drew alongside her flowerbox, it stopped, a window rolled down, and a gloved finger appeared, pointing straight at Renée:

“You! Listen here!”

Rarely had anyone been addressed in such a theatrical manner in the county of ***, especially in broad daylight.

“I’ve heard good things about you.”

The woman's words trailed through her mouth like boots in snow, and yet she chose each one without hesitation.

"I need someone at Spencer Wood for the Turkish baths and other things, to look after my daughter and for a few other odd jobs. You'll do just fine. I'll be expecting you next Monday."

Renée stood there, arms hanging, feeling stupid at having this woman she'd only ever seen two or three times organize her life.

"I know you already work for that man Marquette, but never mind. He'll find someone else, I'm quite sure."

Long after the car had disappeared into the distance, and on into the evening, Sarah Rosenberg's words echoed in Renée's head, right up to the moment she felt herself fall. "I've heard good things about you." She heard it again: "Good things."

23

CELESTE DIDN'T WALK to the spring every day, but when she did, she would pull behind her a wagon loaded with jars and bottles to be filled with its cool, fresh water—Margot swore by the water, claiming it had once cured her of a bad case of whooping cough.

The spring water gushed from between two moss-carpeted rocks at the end of the lane where Bella Webb had built her gloomy house. Celeste waved as she went past. She still had a mile or so to walk.

"Need any water, Bella?"

There was no reply. The widow was stacking firewood near the shed. Celeste envied her strength and powerful build while she, for all her energy and dedication, was more willow than oak. She imagined the strenuous chores she could have accomplished if only she'd been graced with Bella's strapping physique. "She makes good use of it nonetheless; she's almost as valiant..." "As me," she nearly said, holding back only out of a sense of God-fearing humility.

The wagon wheels bumped and rattled over the rutted dirt road, but Celeste enjoyed pulling her wagon and hearing the bottles clink; it reminded her of the jangling harness of a workhorse. "How lucky my Basil is to have such a strong wife." There was more than a little pride in the meals she prepared, the stones she picked from the fields, the fires she lit, the gutters she emptied, the water she drew from the well. The thought that Basil might grow bored or melancholic never crossed her mind: before her stretched a path strewn with chores to be done, and at the end of the path Basil was waiting for her, and he was one more duty, but a kind duty, a rewarding duty. Celeste wouldn't have wanted to be married to any other man; Basil couldn't have hoped for a better woman than Celeste. She could have been more in love, but never could she have been as free; he could have been less alone, but never could he have been better cared for.

Sitting on a rock by the spring, Louise Beurre smoothed her skirt as little droplets bounced off her leather boots. An old woman wrapped in a thick cape sat silently on the other side of the flowing water. So they remained, comfortable, for nearly an hour, perfectly content, until the woman spoke up:

"Miss, do you think you could give me a little water to drink? My back is giving me such trouble, I'm afraid it'll seize up altogether if I try to lean over to drink from the spring."

"I surely would, ma'am, but I didn't bring anything to draw water. I was just passing by."

"Your hands will do just fine, miss."

Louise couldn't begin to imagine this stranger lapping water from her cupped hands. What if her tongue were to touch her skin? What kind of person was she anyway? You couldn't even see her face with her hood pulled up like that.

"Why don't we wait until someone comes by with a jug? We won't be alone for long. There are always people coming and going. Or at least, there used to be, back in the day."

The old woman folded her hands beneath her cloak without a word.

A few minutes later, the rumble of cart wheels announced the arrival of Celeste, and

Louise thanked the heavens when she spotted the jumble of jars and bottles.

"Hello Louise!" called Celeste, with heartfelt joy. "Oh, what a long time it's been!"

The woman in the cape turned her head towards the newcomer and didn't lose a minute:

"Hello madam, do you think you could give me a little water to drink? I am aching so."

"Of course, ma'am, right away!"

Celeste happily grabbed a terracotta pitcher, her nicest one, then rinsed and filled it from the spring. She tipped it up, helping the old woman to drink from it. After five large gulps, the thirsty woman waved the jug away, wiping her mouth on the back of her hand as she adjusted her hood.

"Thank you, madam, you are very kind. Bless you. And *you*"—she pointed a finger at Louise Beurre—"I cast a spell on you."

Holding onto a tree trunk for support, she got to her feet and shuffled off along a faint path into the woods. Louise said:

"I don't really believe in spells."

"You should. I believe in blessings. I've never seen that woman before. She was like a fairy."

"You're just saying that because you're afraid to say 'witch.'"

Celeste looked thoughtful as she watched the old woman disappear into the distance.

"No, not at all. I said 'fairy' because I mean 'fairy.'"

A silence settled over the women as they went about filling all the containers on the wagon. Louise was surprised that Celeste was determined to haul home such a heavy load.

"Are you joking? I could pull two of these!"

Louise didn't believe it for a minute, but she was pleased, nonetheless, to rediscover Celeste's easy-going nature and good humour. The women walked back to the village together, chatting like old friends, and Louise Beurre—formerly known in Paris as Louisa Louis—filled Celeste in on the ten missing years of her story.

When they passed by Bella Webb's house, Celeste said, with a knowing air:

"Apparently Marquette, the pensioner, turned her down. She wanted them to move in together, but I heard he turned her down. At least that's what Old Roux says. And since then, she's been placing ads far and wide, looking for love."

"Hasn't she found anyone?"

"Oh yes, two men showed up here in recent months, one after the other. They only stayed a few days. I'm not sure why, I suppose they weren't suitable. She must have sent them back where they came from."

The two women fell silent for a moment and craned their necks. It was getting dark, and gloomy Bella had gone inside. Smoke furled from the stone chimney.

24

RENÉE LEPINE, as violently as a vase hurled against a wall, woke shouting, battering the mattress with her heels. Just below the surface floated images of Madam de Sainte-Colombe lighting a match and setting fire to the parlour. Her throat raspy, vision blurred, nightgown smelling of smoke, walls stained, and, of course, the carnage of the bookshelves.

She wanted to stand, to finger the fabric of her clothes, to pull at her hair, to reassure herself that she was actually standing in her nightgown in her room in Madam de Sainte-Colombe's house. And standing there alone, in her nightgown, in her room, she said out loud: "I never dream," and it was the first time she'd ever said it. Then, she turned to the bedside table, glanced down at the book her mistress had loaned her, and said to it, "I am absolutely sure of it: I never dream."

She trembled, more from the thought of perhaps having dreamed than from actually having seen Madam de Sainte-Colombe wandering around, eyes glazed, as she set her book collection alight. "My dreams follow me. I've left Madam de Sainte-Colombe behind, even a sleepwalking Madam de Sainte-Colombe. My dreams follow me. But I never dream."

And she left the room, her hesitant steps leading her down the hall to the parlour doorway, where she stopped. The mistress was snoring in her bedroom. The books were dozing on their shelves. Someone had knocked the tin of matches to the floor; the matches were intact, the books were intact. Renée stood there for a long time observing the room, sniffing the air, tugging at her nightgown, eventually realizing that she was standing in a real parlour, wearing a real dress, in the home of a sleeping Madam de Sainte-Colombe. No smoke, no fire, no auto-da-fé.

25

ONE MORNING, two weeks before she disappeared, young Lucy Webb decided to feed some hay to her hobbyhorse. Her father sent her to the next road over, to see Old Mr. Roux, who had a ramshackle shed where he'd always kept a dim-witted donkey. When the donkey would die, he'd buy another one. Sometimes, though not often, he would be spotted riding his donkey, plodding along the local paths. It made a change from his usual, frenzied walking pace.

Damasus Webb said to his daughter:

"Go on, walk down to Old Man Roux's house. He keeps hay for his donkey. Tell him it's for your dolly, and if he says no, give him these," he said, handing her two freshly laid eggs.

"It's not for my dolly. It's for my hobbyhorse."

"Go on, off you go," he said, giving her a little pat on the shoulder.

The child wriggled out of the grasp of her father's grubby hands and skipped off. She slipped the eggs into the pocket of the apron her mother would knot around her waist first thing every morning, although it always looked as if she were tying Lucy to the apron, rather than the apron to Lucy, like a weighty reminder to get to work, to pitch in. The girl was oblivious to her mother's message, and never lifted a finger. That was just fine by Damasus Webb; in any case, he feared what passersby might say at the sight of a seven-year-old girl splitting wood. It wouldn't have gone over well, even in the county of ***.

Lucy Webb scampered alongside the ditch all the way to the crossroads. She tried to gather a bulrush without getting her feet wet, but only managed to pull the top part off, which she squeezed between her fingers, releasing its cottony fluff.

Nobody answered when she knocked on Old Mr. Roux's door. He must have been off on his rounds through the village. The child sat down on a stump in front of the dumb donkey's shed.

"Hey, stupid donkey. What do you think I'm hiding in my apron?"

A wasp buzzed around her tangled hair.

"Oh, you pesky critter!" she cried, repeating the words her mother always shouted whenever an insect flew past.

It wasn't until a half hour later that Old Roux came back from his walk, snuck up behind Lucy Webb and began to tickle her, as furtive as can be. The girl screamed and fell forward, crushing the eggs in her pocket and soiling her apron in the process. Old Roux guffawed while Lucy stamped her feet in anger. Seeing there was no calming the girl's fury, he lost his patience:

"What are you doing at my home, in front of my donkey, anyway, Lucy Webb?"

The child immediately burst into tears.

"Like mother, like daughter! Like mother, like daughter!"

Old Mr. Roux was not the kind of man who could ever understand that for a young empress like Lucy Webb, being compared to her fortress-like mother was nothing short of an insult.

"Go to hell, you old geezer! Go to hell!"

She stretched her hands out in his direction, wiggling her fingers as though playing an invisible piano. "I shall cast a spell on you, Old Man Roux!"

He grabbed her by the arm and scolded her until she sunk her teeth into his elbow, wriggled free, and took off down the road as fast as her legs could carry her.

Bella Webb heard her daughter arriving from afar. When the child came snivelling up the path to the house, the lanky woman grumbled angrily, snatched off the girl's apron, plunged it into a bucket of water, and furiously scrubbed it with soap on the washboard, her eyes never straying from the child.

"Damasus Webb! Your daughter!"

The father appeared from around the back of the house, and when he saw Lucy, her cheeks streaked with tears, he shrugged and led her into the house, leaving Bella to her rage.

26

UNLESS IT WAS RAINING, Louise Beurre would kill at least two hours every day sitting beside the spring at the end of the lane. In the steady trickle of water, she could hear the tick-tock of the clock in her dressing room at the Théâtre de l'Ambigu-Comique. She would drift off into her daydreams and memories, and anyone who stopped by to drink would be met with an impenetrable smile.

"How is it possible to live in the cold and shadow after shining so brightly in the limelight?" This was the kind of question she pondered. She would contemplate at length, perfectly content to let the widow Clot look after the house: she had unearthed an embarrassing secret from her landlady's past and, ever since, she'd been blackmailing her in return for free room and board. Threats, innuendo, whisperings: she'd specialized in such techniques ever since she'd been caught pilfering an umbrella from a boutique in Cherbourg. That's when she'd discovered her second talent, after acting that is, namely lying—although perhaps they were really just one and the same, a talent as puffed up as a festering wound. She didn't reflect; she acted. Except at the Rosenbergs' the other day, when she'd completely unravelled in front of Lisa and her mother.

"How curious," she thought to herself. "My worst audition, by far, and it's for the role of a servant!"

She was hypnotized by the flowing water and she tried to slow time by fixing her gaze on a single droplet. The startling intensity with which she would focus on each droplet, before it was swallowed up by the next, would last for ages.

"My worst-ever audition, and for the role of a servant... I suppose it goes to show I was born to play the role of great ladies."

When it came to questions about her sudden return to the county of ***, the suspicions and rumours surrounding her life as an actress, and her comings and goings after leaving the troupe, she either avoided them altogether or responded with the lies that came so naturally, as she had the day before with Celeste, to whom she'd described a farcical tale in such detail that she'd need the memory of an elephant to repeat the same story twice.

"You know, Celeste, that I left the county to perform with a travelling circus—a real fiasco, to tell you the truth—and that once I arrived in the city, I was invited to join a theatre troupe, a well-known company, a truly exceptional bunch. Then we went to Cherbourg, where we rehearsed until we were ready to move to Paris, to the Théâtre de l'Ambigu-Comique, do you know it? No? It's ever so famous! Very, very well known. You'd love it!"

She pieced her tale together like a leakproof dam, with no regard for the truth, or for the interest of the person she was speaking to, for that matter. She slipped back into a mocking Parisian accent, marvelling at the sound of her own tune:

"There were many of us in the troupe, but I was the star, right from Day One. We performed absolutely everything, the great classics by Molière and Racine. I played Phaedra, Roxane, Esther... Do you know them? No. They're the greatest heroines of French classical drama!

True giants! How I loved playing those roles! We were such a hit in Cherbourg, and even more so in Paris. Even Louis Feuillade came to see me one evening. You do know who Louis Feuillade is, don't you? No. A film director."

Celeste stopped for a moment to catch her breath, and Louise took the opportunity to take a long swig from one of the jugs of water.

"But I grew tired of it. Tired of it all! Of my clothes, my jewelry, my friends... and another actress, an old cretin of a woman who took a dislike to me, trying to extort ridiculous amounts of money from me. The stories people make up! One fine evening, I quit the stage: I'd had enough. I chucked my wings down a hole—I was playing an angel, you see, and I had to wear wings and a frightfully heavy halo, a ridiculous get-up... you would have laughed! Anyway, I grabbed my coat and hat, threw all the costumes, gloves, stockings, and shawls I could lay my hands on into a suitcase, and slipped out the back door. I still had one scene to play! The audience was waiting for the angel to arrive, you see? I was supposed to come down from the heavens and pardon someone, some fellow who had swindled his brother and cheated on his wife. Can you imagine *me* absolving someone of that kind of crookery! No. Well, anyway, it wasn't just that; it was everything.... it was the constant exhaustion, the men, the pressure... So I just left. That very night I took a train all the way to Brest. It's a city, Celeste! A city that feels like the end of the world. I felt as though I were at the end of the world. I found a job, oh it was easy enough. In a very fine cabaret. The Recouvrance, have you heard of it? No. One of Brest's most respectable cabarets. I would sing there twice a day. Oh, the smiles I would bring to the tired faces! I met a man there, you know. A sailor. Now, I know what you're going to say about sailors and seamen..."

Celeste had no intention of saying any such thing.

"Not this one, Celeste. He was a courageous man. Not one to fear an actress, not one to fear a famous woman, I'm telling you. But..."

Here, she paused for a moment, unsure which direction her story would take next.

"But my sailor—a captain, actually, did I mention that already?—he died at sea. It was just like in the song. Do you know it, Celeste? No. The one that goes:

So sang my father as he left the port.
Never expecting his life be cut short.

The winds, the storm, such sudden surprise.
The cruel shipwreck where he met his demise."

Louise Beurre, a.k.a. Louisa Louis, sang loudly. It was something she'd often been reproached for at the theatre: singing at the top of her lungs and drowning out the others. Her bellowing flushed out a couple of partridges from the side of the road, startling Celeste, and a bottle fell from the wagon, shattering on a rock.

"How clumsy!"

The contents of the bottle spilled out, draining away into the ditch, which brought Louise, unfazed by the broken bottle, back to her tale:

"Water! So treacherous. It stole away my captain. And now he sleeps twenty thousand leagues under the sea."

She smiled at her own clever turn of phrase. Celeste ventured a question:

"Were you married?"

"Ye...yess," stammered Louise. "In actual fact, we were."

"He didn't leave you with any debts, I hope?"

Louise was like a waterwheel, spinning tales, tall tales, and Celeste was the water that fed the wheel.

"Oh, all kinds! You see, my captain, he was a gambler. Oh, I was saddled with debt after debt. Years it took me to pay them off! So I sang for two years at the Brest cabaret, then I left for Limoges, and then I went back to Cherbourg,"—by this time, Louise Beurre was growing tired of embroidering her story and she decided to wrap it up. "You see, my dear Celeste, when I returned to the port where I had originally disembarked, all innocence and wonder, my heart melted. And in that puddle of tenderness, I glimpsed my county, my village, my people. And I wanted more than anything to see what had become of you all. But Celeste, what I've told you today, you must keep to yourself, you understand? People are such gossips here. Especially Old Roux. And even Margot..."

While there was nothing especially scandalous about her rambling tale, by entreating Celeste to keep it confidential, she lent it a certain air of credibility.

"Cross my heart," Celeste promised, nearly out of breath.

A silence settled over the women. Celeste could frankly think of nothing else to say, and wondered to herself why Louise was making it all sound so mysterious. So she changed the subject.

"What about Renée?"

At the mention of the name, Louise Beurre flinched from head to toe.

"What about her?"

"You said you wanted to see what had become of us all. Have you seen what has become of Renée?"

Louise suddenly appeared to recall something upsetting, and tears welled in her eyes as she rummaged under her shawl for a handkerchief. Celeste said nothing more, the clinking bottles the only sound disturbing the silence that hung over them the rest of the way back to the village.

"Don't speak to me again about Renée, Celeste. I left thirteen years ago... a lifetime ago! There's my life before"—here, she bent her left arm and opened her palm, as if to offer seed to a bird—"and my life after"—she bent her other elbow and opened her right palm. Celeste could have lifted her by the two handles and filled her like one of her water pitchers. "Two lives! Renée belongs to my life before."

Truth be told, Celeste didn't much care for people's feelings, she was simply keeping the conversation going as best she could. The two women went their separate ways once they reached the house of the widow Clot, who greeted Louise Beurre with a wail: her left foot was turning purple.

27

"MISS LEPINE, we have been eagerly awaiting you. How is it that you have arrived on foot? I sent the driver to get you. Didn't you see him on the road? Ah, you took the footpath. That's at least a two-mile walk. I didn't want you to think me unkind. And that man Marquette who you worked for? Angry? Ah, disappointed? He'll get over it. I've been told good things about you, miss. By whom? By ladies, here and there. You know, I employ only the most discreet people. Spencer Wood is a large house. And in large houses, large and small things alike occur. Things that have no need to be divulged. You understand, I am quite certain. Very well. Lisa will show you to your room. Get settled and get some rest. This evening I will explain everything to you. Your meal will be served at seven o'clock in the kitchen."

Sarah Rosenberg had rattled off her little speech with surprising warmth and kindness, barely stopping to take a breath. Dressed in her usual pearly grey dress, she appeared to float in the middle of the grand foyer where she had positioned herself to greet Renée, like a statue in the park, smack in the middle, in the very centre of the compass pattern set in the marble floor. Her daughter stood to her right, flanked by the yellow dog that never left her side. She reached for the handle of Renée's suitcase, and before Renée could protest, she'd carried the object up to the second floor in a flash, then down two long corridors until they came to a bedroom bathed in light. Young Lisa stuck out her hand for a coin. Disconcerted, Renée rifled through her bag for a penny, but the best she could offer up was an old peppermint.

"Rewards work well with me, Miss Lepine. Very well."

A bird of prey suddenly smacked into the window behind Renée, who let out a shriek. Lisa Rosenberg left the room as though nothing had happened, and when Renée went to the window, she saw that the bird had left a wet mark on the glass.

"Miss Lepine? Where is she? Miss Lepine? Ah, there you are; I didn't see you there. You were so close to the wall. Do you always hug the walls like that? That's good. Very discreet. You haven't eaten yet; your meal is at seven. Lisa and I eat a little later. There are only a few servants. You've met the cook, and I have my maidservant and chambermaid. Then there's the butler, who's also the driver and valet, and a man who comes twice a week to care for the garden. That's all. You will have to work hard! Spencer Wood is a large house. Difficult to maintain. I know that in the village, people don't really know us. We tend to go into the city. We prefer that. You'll get used to Spencer Wood. It's a beautiful property. You'll never be bored. Come!"

Sarah Rosenberg slid her bony hand down the banister as she descended the stairs. Renée followed. They could hear Lisa and her dog taking a bath in a distant room. "Imagine the water everywhere!" Renée thought to herself.

"This is the small parlour. It's where I spend most of my time. I have everything I need here, you see,"—she indicated a table piled high with playing cards, newspapers, spools of thread, and eggshells. “Lisa keeps me company. I give her lessons here, but from now on, that will be your job. No need to supervise her. The dog, who follows her everywhere, is extraordinarily intelligent. You will have only to discipline her as required, and give her lessons in the morning. I expect you to assist my chambermaid Odile, especially for the darning. She is getting old, and her fingers are more gnarled than ever. This is the main parlour; over there is the library. Nothing of interest there. We never use it. And this is the kitchen. You’ve met our cook, Agnes. Here’s the formal dining room, and here is the day-to-day dining room. Of course, I’m showing you all this quickly, because you will have no need to dawdle here. I will show you the upstairs tomorrow. The main thing is to remember how to get to your room. But above all else...”

She stopped abruptly and leaned against a mahogany pillar with a look of crushing fatigue—they were back in the grand foyer.

“There is one special place I must show you.”

She nodded to a door hidden beneath the main staircase.

“It’s over there. Follow me.”

Sarah Rosenberg had begun to whisper now. Renée Lepine followed behind, her arms held stiffly by her sides, until they reached the spiral staircase beyond the door, where the flicker of a candle would have been more fitting to light the stone walls and mould than the single lightbulb that someone had strung from a wire.

"I'll show you downstairs."

Renée felt an increasing sense of dread. She had developed terrible claustrophobia as a child when, at the age of ten, she had been trapped in a cold storage room for two days and two nights.

"Perhaps you've heard about the baths. Or perhaps not. They're a bizarre, exotic thing. I didn't want them; it was my late husband who insisted on acquiring these curios. You feel like you're in the tropics. Or at least, I imagine so. I've never been in them. I prefer the cold, myself. They may not look like much, but they require some maintenance. You won't have to touch them. In any case, no one uses them anymore. You should know that I forbid Lisa from coming down here."

The stone staircase spiralled down until it came to a corridor, also of stone, that was lit, too, by a naked bulb dangling from a wire overhead, and that led to two doors engraved with motifs in the Arabian style. Sarah Rosenberg motioned to them, first to one, then to the other, but didn't open them.

"These are the Turkish baths. They are not working at the moment. No one need go in there. And these are the electric baths. Perhaps you've heard about them. Or perhaps not. I hadn't either. Another one of my late husband's ideas. If I had to describe them, I'd say they are not unlike sarcophagi."

She looked deep into Renée Lepine's eyes as she said the word "sarcophagi."

"They look like sarcophagi. There are two of them. Boxes that you lie inside. There's an electric mechanism that sends heat into the box, so the person starts to sweat. It's a therapeutic procedure that promotes weight loss. My late husband swore by them. You..."

She was backing up without realizing it; as she'd been speaking, she had backed up against the staircase and already had her foot on the first step.

"She clearly wants to get out of this place, and I don't blame her," Renée thought.

"You will be in charge of these baths."

Renée stood taller and clasped her hands together.

"Madam? I thought no one used them anymore."

"Quite so, Miss Lepine. You listened well. You will be in charge of this place in the same way that the driver is in charge of the car, even when no one is using it."

"A symbolic responsibility, madam?"

Sarah Rosenberg pursed her lips; she clearly hadn't hired the most dim-witted woman in the county.

"Not exactly, miss. It is you I will ask to come down here, should I feel so inclined."

"Inclined to use the baths, madam?"

Although Renée knew she was pestering her mistress with her questions, she nonetheless felt a desperate need to understand and, more than that, to hear from her mistress's lips that she wouldn't have to return to this sinister place anytime soon. Sarah Rosenberg was running out of patience, but at the same time, she realized how opaque her explanations were.

"No. Simply feel inclined to have you come. You see, miss..."

"She looks like she's about to strike the final blow," Renée thought to herself.

"In actual fact, you will come down here every evening. At midnight."

Renée felt something catch in her chest and a cold droplet trickle down her spine. Sarah Rosenberg lowered her chin, as if she were about to address the stone floor.

"No doubt you believe I have a Cartesian mind, Miss Lepine. Well, you're right. You're right. And yet, I am asking that you come here every night, at midnight. That you open the doors. Turn on the lights. Go into the rooms. Take a look around. Make sure *everything is normal*. Then, turn off the lights, close and lock the doors, and go back upstairs. This will be one of your chores. In fact, I would say it is your main chore, miss. That's just how it is. I know it may seem fanciful. But I assure you that, on the contrary, it couldn't be more serious."

Sarah Rosenberg's tone suggested that "Why?" would not be part of the discussion.

"Welcome to Spencer Wood," she called back over her shoulder as she made her way up the timeworn stairs from the cellar, then, spotting Renée some five steps behind: "What's the matter with your leg? You're limping."

Renée held a hand to her left hip and then shifted her weight, as if to lean on the walls for support.

"Madam has a keen eye. I contracted polio as a young child."

"Does it hurt? I mean, does it cause you great pain?"

"It's worse in the evenings. I have trouble going up and down stairs."

Renée wanted to find a way out of her extraordinary nighttime duty. Standing perfectly still on the landing, Sarah Rosenberg eyed her with concern; she seemed to be thinking carefully. Alarmed at the hesitation in her eyes, Renée Lepine thought for a moment that she was going to close the door in her face as she stood halfway up the stairs, and leave her with the sarcophagi. When she reached the main floor, she called out:

"It's really nothing, madam. Just a trifle! It will just take me a little longer, that's all."

Which satisfied her mistress.

"Well, that's a relief. Take all the time you need. The main thing is that you do it. It is crucial that you do it."

Back in her bedroom, Renée sat down on the edge of the bed and slowly rubbed her palms together. She would have to go back down to the Turkish baths again that very night, and the following night, and the one after that, too—the very thought of which set her mind spinning.

In the hedge beneath the window, the bird of prey stiffened, its eyes turning glassy.

28

Dear Madam,

While I may not be a big landowner, I am as strong as an ox, and I will do what it takes to protect you. I am looking for a fine little woman to join...

Bella Webb rolled her dark eyes and tossed the letter into the fire as soon as she got to the "fine little woman" bit.

Dear Madam,

My aged father bequeathed his land to me, and I am hoping to sell it and settle in the city. I hear there are good jobs to be had in the offices there. If you are willing to join your destiny to mine, I will take you to the city. I am seeking a country-bred woman to cook me the meals my mother used to make.

More rolling of the eyes. One more crumpled wad of paper.

Dear Madam,

My late wife, who had trouble with her innards, expired last month.

Bella Webb shuddered with contempt and continued reading.

I'm all alone with the ghosts in my big house. I will be happy to correspond with you for just as long as it takes and, if you will have me, to sell my belongings and join you. I'm no King Croesus, but the proceeds from the sale of my land would allow you to rule quite comfortably.

Sincerely yours,
Samuel Tardy

Bella Webb felt a rush of warmth, and her cheeks flushed. The same warmth and the same flush she'd felt with Marcus Pilgrim—since come and gone—and Raymond Chance—who never came at all. And for that other, John B. Mortimer, who had journeyed to the door of his bride-to-be, but had failed to meet with Bella's approval, what with his greasy hair and princely ways.

She straightened her jacket, even though there was no one there to see it in her dark and gloomy kitchen. She sat down at the table beneath the oil lamp and began her fourth letter.

29

LOUISE BEURRE recognized the old woman in the cape who had asked to drink from her hands, like a dog. "Her again!"

The woman squelched towards the spring on the path made treacherous from the recent rains, the mud sucking at her heels. Louise, who'd been lying there on a rock for hours, sat up and shifted her gaze to the dense woods, the indecipherable sadness on her face very much designed to discourage conversation.

The strange woman finally made her way to a stump and sat down, tucking her hands beneath her cloak. She turned to Louise who, determined as she was to focus elsewhere, couldn't ignore the spongy presence, the grey cape that covered her like a mantle, nor the gaping chasm formed by her hood, a black hole that revealed nothing, not even the tip of her nose.

"I remember you. I cast a spell on you."

Louise Beurre started.

"Oh!" as if she'd just noticed she wasn't alone. "What was that you said?"

"I said I remember you. I cast a spell on you."

"Well, I don't know what to say."

The stranger cleared her throat. Then Louise found something to say.

"I don't believe in spells."

"It's not a spell; it's a curse."

"You just said it was a spell."

"It's a curse."

The old woman pulled one hand out from beneath the cape and rested it on the stone in front of her. She had the skin of an iguana, restless fingers with long, curling nails.

"But you can break it."

"I don't believe in curses either."

"But this one can be broken."

Louise Beurre got to her feet and shook out her skirts.

"Well, then. Are you going to tell me what curse you cast upon me?"

Louise suddenly felt faint and nearly fell to the ground. She clasped her hand to her forehead, eyeing the stranger all the while. She wondered if she'd gone crazy, if she was actually talking to a block of granite. The old woman said:

"Don't worry. It's just a little one. Not like the hex I cast on that other woman."

"What other woman?"

"The tall one with the dark hair. It was a powerful hex for her."

"What did she do to deserve that?"

"I saw her mistreating her child."

"Her daughter? She died over a year ago. What did you see?"

"Nothing good. So I bewitched her. She deserved it."

"I don't believe that. You mean Bella Webb? Whatever did you see?"

The woman's other hand reappeared from beneath her cloak, as if disarticulated, the two spider-like hands coming together on the stone in a clicking of nails. Louise shuddered.

"I saw her distend her daughter."

Louise Beurre felt a blast of heat come over her, the words triggering a deep shame. She pinched the skin between her thumb and index finger.

"Really? Well, it can't have been that bad."

Sweat began to bead on her forehead.

"How did you put it again?"

"I said I saw her distend her daughter."

Louise Beurre no longer had any desire to hear or to understand the woman's disturbing choice of words. Her ears were abuzz.

"You say things like that, but surely you don't expect to be understood. You say those things, and then what? You expect me to question you? Well I won't."

The other woman had tucked her hands beneath her cloak once again.

"You wanted to know. And now you don't understand. I saw her distend her daughter."

"That's enough! Or do you intend to repeat those words to Mrs. Webb herself?"

"No need. She already knows. You don't think I can cast a spell from afar? A spell is a matter of words. Nothing more. No magic, no mystery. Just words. Words that slither into your ears. That's all it takes."

Louise Beurre had heard quite enough:

"I've heard more than enough and I'm leaving. And as for my curse..."

The old woman got to her feet as well. Once unfurled, she was surprisingly tall.

“Do you want to know how to break it?”

“I don’t believe in this nonsense. And I suggest you keep your bizarre words hidden under that big cloak of yours. Witch!”

Louise took to her heels as the other woman called after her: “It’s not magic! It’s never been magic!”

30

BELLA WEBB (although the other women in the county would have been surprised to hear it) had a habit of daydreaming. She would stand by her bedroom window, focus on something that caught her attention—a tree, an animal, a shape projected by a flicker of sunlight—and she would wish.

As a young girl, in her native county, she had wished for all kinds of honest things for other people: good health, a bountiful season, warm sunshine, cool rains, abundant harvests for all the farmers in the county, better lungs for her tubercular sister, a few spare coins with which to buy new boots for her good mother, no more runny noses during hay season for her good father, laughter and fun with her friend Lorraine, a long sap-running spring, prosperity, a tranquil and plentiful old age for her parents, with paradise awaiting them at the end of their days.

Now that her parents, sister, daughter, and husband were gone, she wished for things for herself. The kind of man she needed: Not old and frail like Marcus Pilgrim, not temperamental and grubby like John B. Mortimer; a man just like her late Damasus, only more lively, chatty, kind, thin, authoritarian, silent, meek, assertive, strapping, rich, discreet, broad, charming, humble, powerful, serious, timid.

She had wished for reasonable things at the age of sixteen: a decent man, one summer evening when her good mother had allowed her to attend a celebration in the village, a dance where she had drunk one glass, only one, before dancing one dance, only one, with a handsome young man by the name of Poulin, who had smiled at her like no one had ever smiled at her before, had taken her by the hand, had led her outside, beneath a bright moon, had smiled at her again, had pulled her into the dark woods, had hitched up her skirt, had pinched her thighs, had gripped her in his strong hands, had punched her in the gut when she tried to wriggle away, had abandoned her, confused and bruised, in the bushes, had never given her a second thought, had gone off to study somewhere, had become a provincial notary, had married Lorraine, had had five children with her.

"That's all," Bella Webb thought to herself, as she continued to wish, and that summer evening in the year she'd turned sixteen was etched into her wishes. That summer evening in the year she'd turned sixteen tinged her wishes a more vivid and more bloody shade.

These days, she wished as hard as she could for Samuel Tardy who, in his faraway county, at that very moment, was selling his land, loading his belongings onto a cart, emptying his bank account, saying his goodbyes, following the road to Bella Webb's farm; she had written to him, as she had to Marcus Pilgrim, as she had to John B. Mortimer: *Come, and be prepared to stay forever.*

31

RENÉE LEPINE grew thinner by the day, earning her a caustic remark from young Lisa Rosenberg:

"You're thinner than my bicycle, miss. Mother, Miss Lepine is thinner than my bicycle!"

"I, too, am thin, Lisa. Whatever do you mean? One doesn't compare one's governess to a bicycle!"

She was expected to teach the girl subjects that Renée deemed entirely lacking: "Latin and French," "piano," "a few notions of history," "proper etiquette," "embroidery." The second day, when she'd explained to Sarah Rosenberg that she could teach neither piano nor history and that, as for Latin, she knew only the rudiments herself, her mistress had replied, "But etiquette, French, and embroidery you can, isn't that so?" and Renée had replied, "Yes, I can." It seemed that would suffice, after all.

While the mistress demanded little of her daughter, her indulgence reached staggering heights when it came to herself. She could spend ten hours lying on her chaise longue, five consecutive days cloistered in her bedroom, three weeks without leaving the house, two months never venturing beyond the gates of the estate. Every now and again a few city folks would come to visit the Rosenbergs. They tended to be people who were somewhat worn and faded, like a threadbare carpet, probably once-rich families who'd seen better days. Renée Lepine was surprised that such well-off people, to whom the inhabitants of the county attributed all sorts of knowledge and power, could live in such mediocrity.

The midnight rounds, on the other hand, were apparently of the utmost importance, and formed the part of the day around which everything else revolved. Sarah Rosenberg could be heard daily, reminding Renée to go, then roaming the corridors late into the night until the servant had gone down to check the baths, then come back up to announce that "everything is normal," a statement Renée found so enigmatic, so contradictory, considering that, to her mind, there was nothing normal at all about Spencer Wood.

And she continued to grow thinner and thinner. The mere thought of her nightly descent into the bowels of the manor house would cause her heart to start palpitating around noon, dampening her appetite, which only returned during the night, when the cook was fast asleep, so she'd have to make do with a few shortbread cookies she'd fish out of a glass jar.

One morning, Lisa figured out what was causing the dark circles beneath Renée's eyes, her thinness, and the wisps of hair that kept escaping from her bun, and she set out to exploit her advantage.

"Miss Lepine, I know what you're up to."

The girl was kneeling on the carpet in the small parlour, writing a composition, and she addressed Renée without lifting her gaze from the notebook in front of her. Renée was slouched on the sofa, struggling to fend off the slumber that escaped her every night, then assailed her from the first light of dawn.

"You know what I'm up to? Whatever do you mean?"

"I know you're just pretending. You go down into the cellar at midnight, but you don't open the two doors. You just pretend. You wait a minute or two, then you come back up."

Utter lies. Since she'd begun working at Spencer Wood a month prior, Renée had opened each door twenty-nine times, looked inside each room twenty-nine times—always in anguish and terror, if you please. The accusation stung her pride, all the more so since she suddenly realized how extraordinarily stupid it was to obey an order when no one could possibly verify or gauge the result.

"It's impolite to make up stories. I don't have to report to you, Miss Lisa, and even if I did, I would have nothing to be ashamed of. Now, finish your composition."

It was the first time anyone had raised the matter of the baths with her. Renée, by some mystery of self-deception, had come to consider the chore a humiliation. "Ridiculous," she muttered under her breath, as she descended the mouldy stairs to the cellar. "Ridiculous" was an inedible word, but she could think of no other, and once she was back in her bedroom, when she stripped the sheets from her bed, she thought she could see, imprinted on the mattress, the contours of her body, curled into a ball, pressed up against her shame, clutching it tight to its chest the way a child cuddles a teddy bear, and she could have lain down beside it so it could soak up her solitude from the previous night and carry it over into the next.

Of course, she was tormented by questions, but she didn't feel right discussing them with a child. Though Lisa continued:

"I know what's happening to you. I can tell that you aren't sleeping well. My mother has infected you with her insomnia."

The child shifted to a cross-legged position.

"You must be wondering why she asked you to do it. Do you want to know why?"

Lisa held out her right hand.

"If you give me a dollar, I'll tell you."

Renée Lepine leaned over the girl's outstretched hand, as if to read the lines of her palm, and was about to lift her head and pronounce a word that would cut through her shame, but she knew she was fooling herself: shame wasn't a cabbage you could slice in two.

"Don't be naughty, Miss Lisa. What is it with your habit of constantly asking for money! I shall cure you of it!" The girl sensed that her offer had sown a seed in her governess's mind, a seed that would germinate and spread like thrush. Satisfied, she lowered her gaze and concentrated on her homework. Renée sat on the sofa and wrung her hands.

"Surely, not a whole dollar. That's too much."

"That was quick," Lisa Rosenberg thought to herself, blushing with pride.

"Alright, fifty cents, then. I just want to help you, Miss Lepine."

32

"OH NO," Bella Webb muttered, the day after Samuel Tardy arrived at her house. "Oh no," when, as she came in, she saw him sitting by the fire, one hand inside his pants, the other resting on his knee, his eyes like spotlights as he looked her up and down and she, exhausted from her workday, her dress covered in dirt, cheeks flushed from the sun.

He was barely taller than her, with long legs attached to a long trunk topped by a long neck. A tall creature of little appeal, little valor, little interest. Bella already abhorred that tall, slow-moving creature that had brought a measly six hundred dollars into her home.

"I will never marry that. *That* will end up where it belongs," Bella Webb vowed to herself through clenched teeth. She went about preparing the soup in angry silence while Samuel Tardy continued his business, saying only "You don't mind, do you?" in an idiotic, nonchalant tone.

Out of the corner of her eye, she followed the hand as it disappeared beneath the unbuttoned pants in a calculated movement, convinced he was trying to arouse her without frightening or coercing her, but even that restrained and silent motion there in her house, in her home, was frightful and coercive. She couldn't help herself: there was another animal in her lair, and it had to be banished. Her brow furrowed as she prepared the meal, a sadness grasping her by the hair, the embarrassment of having taken this man into her home and of hating him, of wanting to send him packing, the shame of having him leave the village the way he'd come, return to whence he'd come, and yielding his place to another disappointing, abhorrent, unbearable man.

"Give it a few nights. Give yourself a couple more days," she said to herself as she sliced the potatoes, impatience burning her fingers.

Samuel Tardy clucked his tongue and smiled in her direction, growing less inhibited by the minute. He asked the same question once, twice, clearly hoping that Bella Webb would join him "in his filthy ways," she thought.

She set the knife down on the table, looked over towards the rocking chair. The man took her glance for an invitation and lowered his trousers even further, laughing like a child, his movements no longer restrained. "Come here, Bella," he said, patting his lap.

She picked up the knife, set it down again. Picked it up. Set it down.

33

"IT'S BECAUSE OF MY LATE FATHER, David Rosenberg. He died electrocuted in the baths. In the electric baths. And then, a few months ago, my mother woke up in the middle of the night to find herself lying in one of the sarcophagi. She thought she saw my father lying beside her. She never really got over that. So now she needs to take a lot, and I do mean a lot, of precautions. She locks her bedroom door, she locks the cellar door, she locks the doors to the baths, and she has them inspected every night. It helps her to fall asleep."

The child fell silent and went back to her composition.

"Is that it?"

"That's it. Isn't it enough?"

Renée regretted handing over her money.

"Oh, I see. You mean it's not enough for fifty cents?"

"Why doesn't your mother just get rid of the baths?"

"That's a good question, Miss Lepine. You're the first who's dared to ask it. It's not surprising that people say good things about you in the county."

Every time she heard those words, Renée would tumble into them as if into a pile of autumn leaves. They would stick to her clothes, and she wished she could bury herself in them so she'd never hear any others, save for: "They say good things about you."

"She keeps the baths because she's superstitious. She'd probably deny it, but she believes all kinds of stories. She believes practically everything she reads. She's afraid of my father's ghost. She's afraid he'll turn nasty. She doesn't want to set him off. In other words, to keep him content, we can't change anything at Spencer Wood. If you ask me, part of her is dead already. She looks like a ghost, don't you think? Her friends do, too. It's their stillness that makes them so pale and grey. They all think the slightest movement will trigger a catastrophe."

Renée Lepine was startled by the expression, which reminded her of something, but she couldn't quite put her finger on it.

"You..."

Lisa Rosenberg whispered.

"You haven't seen anything out of the ordinary, have you?"

The servant shook herself and straightened, recovering her verve:

"You were the one, Miss Lisa, who accused me earlier of not so much as opening the doors."

"Oh, it was just to see your reaction. So, have you seen anything?"

Renée's tone hardened.

"Don't be ridiculous. Now finish your composition. In any case, I'm lucky, because I never dream."

"But whoever said anything about dreaming?"

That night, Renée Lepine, lying on her cast-iron bed beneath her white sheets in her room in Spencer Wood, didn't fall asleep until long past midnight, her rounds of the Turkish baths having filled her mind with fears from the past that had doubled in volume since hearing Lisa Rosenberg's fifty-cent tale.

The conversation, one precise sentence in that conversation, "He died electrocuted in the baths," had taken root somewhere deep within her, and had come back to her once silence fell, once the darkness enveloped her room, once the chair became a silhouette of a crouching figure, and once the flower buds on the tapestry opened to reveal gleaming eyes. And Renée Lepine was transported to years past, to the gloomy apartment of Madam de Sainte-Colombe, hidden beneath the sheets, her mind haunted by specters, horses, and spiders.

To calm herself before descending into the cellar, she had settled on the unthinkable: she was going to reread *The Science of Dreams*, terrifying though it might be, because it calmed her, because there was nothing more sinister than the underground baths, because nothing chilled her blood more than the image of the man electrocuted to death in the electric baths.

As she felt herself fall. For once, she thought she felt a dream brush past, and before her eyes there marched the battalion of reassuring words she mobilized more than ever, in daytime as in nighttime: "Of course not, I never dream. I never dream."

34

"OH, LOUISE BEURRE! Oh, all the blessed saints up on the clouds in heaven, it hurts so!"

The old widow Clot groaned and lamented and whimpered; her cries had woken Louise in the middle of the night, the bed sheets piled at her feet, the left of which was entirely black, the skin on her leg deformed into a long ridge rising from a wound that glimmered ruby red.

"I'm going to fetch the doctor."

Eva Clot mumbled something that resembled a "yes." Through her sobs came a noise that sounded like that of a groundhog whose den has been walled in.

Louise Beurre threw a coat over her nightgown and pulled on her boots, grumbling all the while as, ever since the incident with the bucket, she'd been telling the widow to have her foot seen to, but the woman's prudishness had gotten the better of her, disguised beneath a façade of "It's not that bad, I can live with it, it only looks like that because it's starting to heal, underneath it's new skin."

Louise went first to knock at Margot's door, to ask her where the doctor lived, and when Margot heard the news of Eva Clot's ghastly complaint, the storekeeper grabbed her jacket and joined Louise, not wanting to miss out. On the way, they were joined by Ginette, who was still suffering from a backache, then when they got to Celeste's house, they decided it wouldn't be right to leave her out. Once Celeste joined their ranks, Margot broke away from the peloton to fetch Bella Webb, who she knew would never forgive them from being excluded from such a squadron. "If only Renée Lepine still worked for Marquette," Ginette noted, but Spencer Wood was really too far. After all, they needed to look after the widow Clot, said Louise Beurre, who harboured not the slightest desire to run into Renée in such circumstances.

The five women advanced like a swarm through the murky shadows of the backroads, chatting as they went. Ginette had already forgotten about the poor woman writhing in pain in her damp bed not far from there.

The doctor had left his home an hour earlier to assist a woman in the neighbouring village who'd gone into labour. Their luck was out, but he would be advised to go straight to Eva Clot's house the minute he got back, they were told. Should the priest be summoned too? "No, there's surely no need for that!" the women exclaimed, as they continued on their way.

They decided they'd better head off to be with Eva Clot, whose wails assailed them the moment they entered the house. "Is she as bad off as that?" asked Ginette, who'd only been apprised very briefly of the situation. Louise Beurre nodded gravely, "It's not a pretty sight, ladies, not for the faint of heart." She looked straight at Ginette and Margot, but Bella Webb brushed aside the warning with a jab to Celeste's ribs:

"Nonsense! I reckon we've seen worse."

And they all made a beeline for the bedroom, Bella in the lead, then Celeste, Louise, Ginette, and Margot, her hand held up to her face, ready to clap it over her eyes.

"Louise, Louise Beurre, is that you?"

The widow Clot cast a feverish glance around the room, and when she saw the foreboding figure of Bella Webb appear in the doorway, lit by the flicker of candlelight, she let out a girlish shriek:

"It's the Purple Hag come to get me! The Purple Hag is going to distend me!"

Louise Beurre stopped in her tracks, suddenly feeling chilled to the bone. That word again, "distend," the same one the old woman in the cloak had used. She waited behind Bella, who propped her hands on her hips and sighed, "She's obviously delirious."

The five women formed a crown around the bed, Celeste lit an oil lamp, and they stayed that way, gathered around the ill woman, who writhed in mounting agony. Margot shed a tear; she'd never seen such necrotic tissue, such a gangrenous limb. "What was she thinking! What was she thinking!" Celeste repeated, biting her lip. Ginette sat down on the edge of the bed and mopped the widow Clot's brow. After a moment, Bella Webb grew impatient.

"If the doctor doesn't get here soon, you know what we'll have to do."

Margot started. "What?"

"Distend her?" Louise thought, filled with dread.

"We'll have to help her. You see that?" Bella continued, pointing to the black foot, "That's dead flesh. There's nothing anyone can do. The doctor will tell you as much: the only thing to do is to cut it off. As for the rest of the leg, well, he'll have to see whether he can save it, but the foot may well need to be cut off."

"What do you mean 'cut off?' *Cut off?* Cut off with what?"

Louise Beurre couldn't believe her ears.

"With a saw, of course. A dried-out leg is just like a log. There's nothing especially complicated about it."

Bella Webb spoke with such assurance that everyone fell silent. The diagnosis, delivered by a simple farm woman—albeit a strong, determined, robust woman, but a farm woman nonetheless—settled like dust in the room, blinding the four women who were all starting to feel queasy from the nauseating heat and the late hour, all except for Bella, that is, who couldn't have been more cool-headed.

An hour went by, Bella's words passing from one mouth to the next, until they lost their meaning entirely. "It may well need to be cut off, if the doctor doesn't get here soon, it may well need to be cut off." Even Ginette, usually the timid one, was swishing them around her mouth, and by four o'clock, with still no doctor in sight, and feeling more dismayed than ever by the sound of Eva Clot's bleating, they finally set their reservations aside, and it was most likely Bella Webb herself, or perhaps Margot or Ginette, who broke the ice and declared, in the irritated tone of a housewife tired of waiting for her guests to arrive before popping the roast in the oven, "It'll have to be cut off, the doctor's not coming, it'll have to be cut off." They were aware sunrise was imminent, could already imagine the busy day that awaited them.

Celeste and Louise continued to resist, feebly, saying, "The doctor's coming. The doctor will save her foot," which Bella rejected with a snort.

Five o'clock came and went, the shadows beneath the trees growing ever longer, the bedroom taking on a pinkish hue that hinted the patient's foot, the patient's leg, once lit by the light of day, would reveal details the night had concealed, details that would be hard to bear.

So, together, the five women brandished those words that would bring an end to the night at the widow Clot's: "It has to be cut off. It has to be cut off now."

35

THE DAY OF HER DISAPPEARANCE, which coincided with her father's, young Lucy Webb woke at dawn and was amusing herself willing a droplet of dew that hung from a branch outside her window to fall. She imagined it falling, but since the droplet remained firmly attached, the girl fell back to sleep in disappointment until her mother brought her her medicine.

Lucy Webb had been suffering for the past couple of weeks from what the doctor called "gastric fever," a name that, in her child's mind, carried neither the gravity nor urgency of the other diseases she'd heard her mother use in reference to various dead acquaintances: "Spanish flu," "cancer," "smallpox," and the worst of all—

because it sounded like it was from another planet—"cholera."

Her ailment was serious nonetheless, and the doctor had warned Bella and Damasus Webb to be prepared for the worst. While the father collapsed into a deep, premature grief, the mother refused to make any concessions, working at the store on Fridays, playing belote, keeping an eye on her daughter as usual, stuffing her with cornbread, potatoes with butter, and lard, and administering her remedy thrice daily.

It wasn't long after ingesting the first dose of medicine, one uncertain morning as sweeping daubs of yellow and pink still hung in the sky, that Lucy Webb's condition took a sudden turn for the worse. Her Damasus of a father was gripped by panic, because the doctor had never categorically condemned their daughter who, only the day before, had been playing at building a wooden shelter for her dolly. But husky Bella took the news in her stride, squeezing the child's hand and whispering words of comfort while Damasus drenched Lucy's arm in a torrent of tears. Torn between summoning the doctor and priest to attend his daughter, but not wanting to leave her side lest she slip away in his absence, the father whimpered like a puppy. An hour later, after an especially painful episode, their Lucy suddenly blanched and dropped her mother's hand, and a long breath, the rattle of which clearly suggested it wouldn't be followed by another, left her still-pink lips.

Just before noon, Bella Webb hitched the horse to the wagon and rode off to fetch the undertaker. A man of a most jovial nature, he nevertheless presented his deepest condolences to Bella.

When they returned to the house, they were met by Damasus Webb, in a state more elongated, more drawn out, more sagging, and heavier than ever, his head down, eyes still swollen in grief, swirling slowly like a wobbly top, hanging by his neck from the rafters.

36

"AND IF THE DOCTOR hadn't arrived, if the baby born to the woman in the next village had been breech, if it had been rainy and stormy, if Bella had insisted even harder, then... then," thought Louise Beurre, as she sat by the spring, "then we would have cut it off."

The shame of having taken part in such a disgraceful rite, one akin to a black mass, gnawed at her, and she wondered what was going through the minds of the other four women, except Bella Webb, who, Louise was quite sure, was going about her business without a shred of remorse.

In the end, the doctor had knocked on the door just as Bella had gone out to fetch her saw; shocked by the state of the widow Clot, he had given her a sedative and immediately driven her to the hospital. When Bella Webb returned, thc light of day and the empty bed, around which Louise, Celeste, Margot, and Ginette were still gathered, seemed to mock their ghastly early morning trance. Bella looked astonished and demanded:

"What have you done with her? Where did you put her? Have you hidden her? There's no point hiding her. It's not a big house, and it's not a big village. It's not even a big county!"

Louise had flinched at Bella's reaction: she saw her now for the madwoman she was, and was surprised that no one had ever noticed the darkness in her eyes, two deep wells that, like death itself, swallowed everything without so much as the echo of a tossed pebble, and she congratulated herself on her keen intelligence, which she immediately put down to her thirteen years in exile. She considered herself well above the Ginettes of the county, could feel the wings sprouting from her shoulder blades, the crown perched atop her head. In her fit of ego, she had forgotten that her newfound mistrust had been cast on her by the old woman in the grey cloak, with the nonchalance of a spider spinning its web to catch the fly.

"We didn't hide her. The doctor took her away."

The farm woman's face had dropped when she heard the good news. "Ah, that doctor," she'd replied. "As unreliable as the weather!" Ginette had sighed in relief, and all the women had trooped out of the house in silence, gone their separate ways, and rushed back to shut themselves away in their homes, all except Louise Beurre, that is, who remained behind at Eva Clot's house, staring at the pile of damp sheets, a pale reminder of their recent nightmare.

The widow did in fact have her foot cut off, although the deed was done at the hospital by a trained surgeon, which prompted Bella Webb to declare that she "would have done just as good a job, only cheaper." Since then, they'd had no news, good or bad, about the poor woman's condition.

And so, Louise Beurre sat by the spring, unsettled and distressed, wishing that the woman in the cloak would suddenly emerge from the bushes. She wanted to tell her she was right, to learn more, as perhaps it was not beneath the old woman's grey hood that the mystery resided after all, but rather in Bella Webb's cottage.

But the stranger didn't come. Instead it was Renée Lepine who appeared, blushing from head to toe at the sight of her long-lost friend and repeating the words that Old Mr. Roux had stolen from her that day beneath her window box: "My heart has stopped," she said to Louise Beurre. "My heart has stopped," but the sound of the gushing water drowned her out.

They had to wait until the spring water hardened like plaster, until the wind died down, until time stood still, because Renée Lepine's heart had stopped, and Louise Beurre, more annoyed than embarrassed, was unable to find the words to start it up again. In the end, her reply was uninspired. She simply said:

"Renée! What are you doing here?"

"It's my day off. I was just out for a walk."

And she found a rock to sit on near Louise, but not too near.

"I'm just back from Celeste's. Eva Clot is not doing so well, I hear. She should have listened to you..."

Renée Lepine was trying to be chummy, but it rang hollow, and she knew it. She searched for something else to say, something that was neither too true nor too banal.

"Do you miss her?"

"Do you miss me?" was what she really wanted to ask.

Louise exclaimed:

"Who? Eva Clot? Certainly not! I keep on her good side because I need somewhere to live, you know. I don't have much to do with her, nor she with me. I just need to find something to do... I need to find something."

She chewed at her fingernails.

"You know, I'm at Spencer Wood now. Mr. Marquette would surely take you on if you're looking for work."

"Yes, that's a possibility..."

Louise Beurre was dreaming of regrets, of vague and fanciful projects a million miles from Marquette the pensioner, while Renée Lepine was attempting to hatch a plan to build something to share, simply, something with which to fill the conversation. She'd intended to suggest that Louise talk to Marquette, and now she'd said it. She wished she could have repaired what was wrong in their lives. She wished they could have been together again, somewhere.

But her wishes were one-sided, because Louise's only desire was to ride off again on a circus wagon, and to be promised the moon by a man in a hat.

She got to her feet. Renée followed suit, and the two women walked back towards the village. When they passed by Bella Webb's cottage, Louise Beurre couldn't resist saying: "Bella Webb is the real witch in this county." The words embedded themselves in Renée's mind, and she didn't dare ask who, in that case, was the phony witch in the county.

A particularly apt gust of wind caught Louise's bonnet and blew it straight into the yard of the sinister farm woman. Louise bit the inside of her cheek: "It doesn't matter, I've got others," she said as she turned for home.

Renée, of course, went back to fetch the hat. It had landed on top of a knotty root protruding from the soil. Renée leaned over and picked it up and, as she straightened, she raised her eyes towards the brilliant sun. There was no tree at the end of the root.

37

RENÉE LEPINE PORED OVER every ad she could get her hands on, every news clipping and magazine, and on her days off, she would walk to the village just to read the noticeboards and search the storefronts for job openings. While many a woman would have been delighted to have her position at Spencer Wood, every night was hellish for Renée, her insides twisting into knots, and Lisa Rosenberg's smirks did nothing to improve matters. One morning, the girl said, in front of her mother:

"Did you enjoy your walk last night, Miss Lepine?"

Since neither woman understood what she meant, Renée queried, "Walk, Miss Lisa?"

"I saw you go downstairs around three o'clock. I should say, I heard you leave your room and I saw you go down the stairs. I saw Miss Lepine go downstairs last night, Mother."

"I heard, Lisa. Miss Lepine must have gone downstairs to fetch a glass of water."

"No, I assure you, madam, I did not leave my room, except at midnight, for the baths. I slept well all night long."

"Well then, you were sleepwalking," spit Sarah Rosenberg. "I cannot abide sleepwalking!"

"I assure you: I do not sleepwalk. I never dream!"

Young Lisa, who was positively glowing by now, added:

"Ah, but that's besides the other night last week, when I saw you from my window walking through the flower beds and disappearing under the big willow!"

Sarah Rosenberg gasped:

"In the middle of the night?"

"Yes, past midnight. It was the middle of the night."

"In her nightgown?"

"Yes, Mother. In her nightgown. With boots on her feet, but in her nightgown."

Renée Lepine had to grab hold of a dresser so she wouldn't deflate like a balloon. Lisa's accusations were, she would have sworn, all lies, and besides, she never went out at night. In fact, if only she could never leave her room at night again, and she mumbled, "If only I could never leave my room at night again." She was referring to the Turkish baths, but the Rosenberg women heard her and took it for a confession.

"Sleepwalking is a disease. We shall have to cure you of it."

"Madam Rosenberg, I assure you, I never dream."

"I'm not talking about dreams, Miss Lepine."

Ever since that conversation, Renée began to think of Spencer Wood as her Gomorrah, and decided to flee, fearing that were she to return, she'd be turned into a pillar of salt. She weighed the two options: either Lisa Rosenberg had fabricated the story entirely for her mother's benefit, or, in actual, terrible, fact she did sleep-walk at night and—without a doubt, because she could have sworn it had never happened to her before—it was because of her torment, because of her midnight rounds. Either way, she opted to flee. Not far, because she was destined to die in the county of ***, but flee she did, all the same.

After leaving Louise Beurre and her bonnet at the widow Clot's house, Renée wandered through the village streets, pondering and reflecting on their bygone friendship. "Could it really have been reduced to water under the bridge? Where were the snows of yesteryear?" The sort of futile questions born of her melancholy nature. She slowed her pace as she reached the home of Marquette the pensioner, the pansies had wilted and shrivelled right down to their roots, and when Marquette appeared in the window and saw her, he pulled the curtains shut with an unequivocal yank.

With every closed door she encountered in the village, she became ever more convinced of the indifference people felt towards her, poor Renée Lepine with her gammy leg, forever drifting from one job to the other, she who, while one of them, lived like a wallflower, born of a mother and father whose appearance and occupation no one could recall. Even Ginette, who was considered rather insignificant, got invited here and there, for no seemingly good reason.

Sarah Rosenberg had managed to pull the wool over her eyes with those beguiling words: "I've heard good things about you." But it was clear, no one had anything to say about her.

Renée finally stopped in front of Margot's store, thinking, "It's been such a long time, and the other night, belote night, it all went quite well," and she decided to go in.

It was a Friday, just past noon, Bella Webb was leaning on the counter, Celeste—because since the night at Eva Clot's place, Margot had been holed up in her home, haunted by visions of amputated feet—was emptying a crate of apples onto a stall.

"Renée! Oh, come on in, have a seat! Bella? It's Renée!"

Bella Webb replied, first with a sullen, "I know, I saw her," then with a slightly less sullen, "How are things at Spencer Wood?"

"Oh, alright."

She instantly regretted not being able to think of anything else to add. But Celeste carried on without picking up on Renée Lepine's discomfort:

"Just alright? I would have thought you'd be well treated by the Rosenbergs. When I go to help out, they always provide a meal. Those

Jews are good payers! I hope you're not sorry you left Marquette the pensioner? I get the feeling he's none too happy with you, but don't worry about him. He's such a miser. He's probably glad to be saving a little money."

Renée walked over to the counter as Celeste finished arranging her apples, came out from behind her cash register, and exclaimed:

"Good Lord, how thin you are! Are you sure you're alright? Bella, look how thin she is!"

Renée struggled to hold back her tears:

"Oh, you know... I don't really like it much at Spencer Wood. It's a strange place. Madam Rosenberg has some unusual habits, and I'm having a hard time getting used to them. You wouldn't believe the things she has me do. The young mistress is also rather troublesome. And it's so big, so cold. And it's a ways from the village."

"So, you'll be quitting then?" Bella asked.

"I don't know. I don't know where I'd go. To the city? There's nowhere left for me here. Unless Margot takes me back at the store..."

Bella hid a frown; she hated Renée's defeatism, her barely concealed complaints, her manner of speaking, as if fate always threw more obstacles in her path than in anyone else's... Celeste didn't seem to notice:

"Of course, if Margot could take you back, that would be ideal. Poor Margot, she's having a terrible time getting over the events of the night... I mean, of that night."

Bella Webb knit her brow at the mention of their ordeal; she was still convinced that, come midnight, they should have gone ahead without waiting for the doctor and cut it off.

38

"MADAM DE SAINTE-COLOMBE, it's Renée. Renée Lepine, do you remember me? I lived with you for a few months. But that was more than ten years ago. Perhaps you don't remember. I know I didn't stay for long. I would have liked to, I was quite happy in your home, but I couldn't stay. You see, you used to dream such a lot. You would dream and you would sleepwalk. I don't know if you ever realized it. I never had the chance to tell you. Because one morning, I simply got up and left. The night before, you were sleepwalking. I tried to wake you, madam. It's hard, you know, and perhaps even a little dangerous. Waking the dead. Sleepwalkers! I meant to say 'sleepwalkers.' The day before, you'd loaned me a book. I must admit, madam, it struck me as odd the way you spent your life with your nose in your books. But I got used to it and, in the end, I understood. I understand now. Anyway, it wasn't a very long book, wasn't even a very good book. But it was the only book you ever loaned me. Do you remember what you said to me one fine evening? When you wished me 'good night,' you said: 'Sleep well, I hope you don't dream.' You were right, as always. We sleep best when we don't dream. Now you're gone, but you left me that book. I'm quite sure you left me it intentionally."

She pulled *The Science of Dreams* out of her bag and leaned it up against the tombstone.

"It was a strange gift, Madam de Sainte-Colombe. Especially for someone like me who never dreams. You know, I was terrified I would be pursued by dreams when I left you. Because that night I saw you—I swear, I saw it with my own eyes—I saw you set fire to your books. I know it sounds absurd. But you were asleep, madam. Perhaps there was something in you that wanted to burn all those books. When I woke up, it was morning. I don't know what happened, or how it happened. I woke up in my room, and the bookshelves were intact. All the books were there. They accused me of sleep-walking, just like you. I wasn't able to explain it. I never dream. And I keep repeating those words, morning, noon, and night. But perhaps they're not the right words after all."

39

OLD MR. ROUX SNATCHED UP THE TRAGEDY of the widow Clot as though pocketing an apple from a fruit stall. With a few embellishments here and there, he set the thrillingly horrific scene, causing the ladies of the Christian Reading Circle to shudder in fright: "Just imagine, Bella had the blade of the saw pressed up against poor Eva's leg, she could feel the metal teeth sinking into her flesh, and it was at that very moment that the doctor rushed into the room, grabbed the saw, and rescued the widow from the clutches of the Purple Hag."

The last known words to leave Eva Clot's lips wormed their way into every home in the county ("It's the Purple Hag come to get me! The Purple

Hag is going to distend me!"). Now every last person knew about the Purple Hag and her sangfroid. The words even reached Spencer Wood where, unsurprisingly, Sarah Rosenberg expressed her admiration for Bella, lauding her detachment and firmness, as if to say "quite the opposite of you," or at least that's how Renée Lepine interpreted it.

Renée left the manor house one rainy afternoon, more exhausted and emaciated than ever, with Celeste, who had come to help her pack her suitcase and load it on her wagon, which she pulled, just like her bottles and jars, all the way to the village.

"Now then, tonight you'll have a good meal, we'll play belote at Louise's place and, starting tomorrow, you'll begin work at the store! Isn't that wonderful? You'll see, everything will work out fine."

Because Celeste, feeling sorry to see Renée more depressed and helpless than ever, had decided to give her a few of her own shifts at Margot's store. The boss didn't know about it. In any case, it was feared she'd lost her mind completely after being traumatized by the foot that once belonged to the widow Clot, who was still being held hostage in hospital by the surgeon.

"Bella Webb's going to take you in. You'll see, it's nice over at her place. And since Damasus and Lucy died, there's plenty of room."

Renée Lepine couldn't care less where she was to be sent. So long as it meant putting as many miles as possible between the electric baths and herself, between the shame, the dreams, the long sleepless nights, and herself.

40

"BELOTE AT LOUISE'S PLACE" was a way of avoiding having to say "Belote at Eva Clot's place," of leaving their fearful memory buried in the soft earth where it had been sleeping for the past week. The widow Clot's place had become Louise Beurre's place for all of the women, and from then on, no further reference to the poor woman crossed their lips.

The black kings were set aside; the teams were formed. Bella and Renée, Celeste and Louise; two hopelessly mismatched pairs: Celeste always passed, and Louise was a poor player, while Bella always took the trump and Renée was the best card counter of the bunch, meaning they won handily and quickly, in sovereign silence.

With each glass of raspberry liqueur, Louise Beurre transformed a little more into Louisa Louis. By nine o'clock she was more than a little tipsy, dropping her cards and giving away her good cards at the most inappropriate moments, which annoyed patient Celeste no end; she wasn't playing to lose, after all. Louise blurted out whatever crossed her mind, further intoxicated by the violent solitude that had gripped her since the hospitalization of Eva Clot, much like the wasting effect of alcohol on an empty stomach:

"So, Bella, I hear the old woman in the cape cast a spell on you?"

Her head bobbed up and down and she played her cards without even looking at them.

"That's what she said."

Renée Lepine, who was disquieted by Louise's behaviour, tried to steer the conversation elsewhere:

"Don't be silly, Louise. I pass."

"She's a stranger! Who wears a big grey cape. Who I see at the spring sometimes. I don't even know what she looks like. But she casts spells. She cast a tiny one on me, but she cast a great big one on Bella, 'the tall, dark-haired one,' she called her. Pass!"

Renée held firm:

"I don't believe in magic."

"But that's just it, Renée. It's not magic. It's just words. That's what she told me."

A cloud of confusion hung in the air and Bella Webb remained silent, her deep gaze flickering from one face to the next. Then she said:

"Louise Beurre, you can't hold your alcohol. You remind me of Eva Clot. She was delirious the other night, spouting all kinds of nonsense. I'll take spades."

Celeste squirmed at the mention of the amputated widow. Louise would surely have reacted were it not for the alcohol. Renée Lepine didn't flinch.

"I'm not delirious. The old woman in the cape, she lives near the spring. She told me things. She used that same word as the widow Clot: 'distend.'"

Bella Webb didn't even lift her gaze from her cards. Renée blushed. Louise shuddered. The drink had made her bolder. They played their hand quickly, a glimmer of sobriety flickered in Louise Beurre's mind, and she fell silent. The bottle of liqueur was empty.

A bird alighting on the windowsill that evening would have seen that Bella Webb had not a single spade in her hand.

41

THE COUNTY OF ***, it is worth mentioning, sits on a fertile stretch of land dotted with innumerable forests of modest size, but with tree trunks so high, so grey, so hard, so dense, that the task of clearing them had long caused much hardship for the good-willed women and men who lived there.

Bella Webb was an ill-willed woman; her Damasus of a husband and she had ripped out hundreds of trees from their parcel of land. All that was left were a few stands of straggly firs, because the sombre woman had a liking for conifers, "trees that never expose themselves."

Renée Lepine, Celeste, and Bella left Louise Beurre's place just before eleven o'clock, made their way through the village, stopped at the edge of the forest, the rumbling sound of thunder fast approaching. Celeste whistled:

"I'll take the trail! With the storm on the way, it'll be faster."

Renée Lepine looked towards the dark trees:

"Celeste... what trail? I can't see any trail in there."

"Don't worry, I always take it. I never lose my way."

Renée shivered:

"I would never be so bold."

And Celeste, the only one to see the irony in the situation, was on the verge of telling her the story of that sleepwalking episode in the woods and the fright it had given them, her and Basil, but a cold, heavy rain suddenly began to fall. Celeste dashed off into the darkness without another word, and Bella and Renée walked on briskly.

Long, white, jagged flashes of lightning zigzagged in the sky. At Spencer Wood, Sarah Rosenberg couldn't sleep, terrorized by the lightning and rain, a troubling combination that evoked in her mind all the bizarreness of the electric baths, of what was slumbering two storeys below, beneath her feet, and that would perhaps awaken, would certainly awaken, if the thunder rumbled any louder.

Renée Lepine and Bella Webb arrived at the log house at the peak of the storm. Renée noticed, while Bella was shaking out her skirts, a little gully of water flowing towards a clump of blue spruce on the far side of the yard, and at the exact moment Bella opened the door to the house, a flash of lightning lit up the scene, revealing, hidden among the trees, what Renée took to be several horseless carriages, three derelict carriages, and a shapeless pile of something animal-like, manes, hoofs, but just then Bella lit an oil lamp and pulled her guest inside.

42

"YOU'LL SLEEP HERE. It used to be Lucy's room. The bed is small, but it's all I've got."

Bella Webb taking in Renée Lepine, Bella Webb housing Renée Lepine under her own roof: Even Old Roux couldn't have dreamed up such an unlikely scenario.

"In any case, you never sleep, do you?"

Deep down, Bella Webb was enjoying having Renée close at hand and close beneath her roof.

"I never sleep? Who told you that?"

Renée was afraid of Bella, always had been, but she was less afraid of Bella than she was of Spencer Wood and its electric baths.

"I thought the Rosenbergs let you go because you were wandering at night, like a ghost."

"I never wander. And nobody let me go. I left of my own accord."

Bella Webb stayed in the room while Renée unpacked her bag, eyeing her with the same look she sometimes gave to her Lucy—impenetrable and volcanic, defiant.

They prepared for bed in monastic silence. Renée Lepine stared out the window, at the same branch that Lucy Webb had once stared at and, this time, the droplets of water hanging from it fell. And Renée, too, felt herself falling.

It was Madam de Sainte-Colombe's sepulcher. The words engraved on the tombstone were slowly fading, as if the rock were claiming back what was rightfully its own, and Renée had to squint to read the words, but all she could see was a hard, symmetrical phrase featuring those words that Louise Beurre had pronounced: "The real witch in this county."

Then, everything changed, the stone grew smooth and wide, taking up all the space, and Renée could feel it in her mouth, in her ears, under her arms, as if it were being placed there. She felt a stone tent rising above her, then crushing her, and she opened her eyes, stunned but still drowsy.

Bella Webb was woken by the sound of Renée's footsteps, uneven like Morse code, stuttering off towards the staircase. "What is she doing up at this hour?" she wondered as she crept out of her bedroom, attempting to make herself as invisible as possible—or as invisible as her brutish size would allow—and followed her guest, who had disappeared into the shadowy darkness of the cellar. "She's wandering, I knew she'd be nothing but trouble. She's wandering just like she did at Spencer Wood, snooping around, poking her long nose into things that don't concern her. She's going to have to be silenced."

Renée reached the bottom of the stairs, sat down, and ran her fingers over the dirt floor of the cellar, like a child at the beach. She collected smooth, white pebbles, pebbles she feared she might eat, might bite down on, might break her teeth on.

She was crawling on all fours when her hand brushed up against a pointy lump in the dirt. Another pebble? No. She tried to pick it up, but it wouldn't budge. She dug around it, it still didn't come free, it was very small on top and very big underneath.

Bella Webb stood hidden in the corner, petrified at the sight of Renée Lepine gradually unearthing a toe, a foot, the tip of an iceberg buried beneath the log house: "She's going to have to be silenced, she's going to have to be silenced," Bella repeated to herself.

When she woke, Renée was lying in her bed.

There she saw, leaning over her, the round face and dark eyes of the towering Bella Webb, who was watching her, a candle in one hand, her other hand clutching her neck; her hair loose and floating around her head, a thick haze hanging in the room. Renée spotted through the doorway the flicker of flames, and imagined she was back at Madam de Sainte-Colombe's house, the smoke, the fire, the dream. Then, Bella placed the candle on the table, sat down on the edge of the bed, silent, powerful and, all soil and embers, wrapped her arm, the arm of a bear, around the neck of Renée Lepine, who opened her pebble-filled mouth as wide as she could, seeking, not finding, wanting, not managing, to cry out, to scream, to drive away her paralyzed, strangled, walled-in nightmare.

43

THE STORM HAD BEEN RAGING FOR HOURS, dawn had been timidly emerging from behind a curtain of rain, sand, and dead leaves that would have discouraged even the most determined of Celestes. Louise Beurre, stage name Louisa Louis, had given up trying to sleep: "At this hour, might as well get up." Her cheeks puckered from the raspberry liqueur of the previous night, her ears still ringing with the sound of her own inebriated voice and the brazen accusations she had levelled at Bella Webb during their game of belote.

She walked past the forbidden bedroom of Eva Clot and headed for the kitchen, but the flicker from her candle wasn't enough to light the bucket, the widow's bucket, lying on the floor, and she stepped straight into it with her left foot, which immediately got stuck in a dreadful cracking of toes. She cried out, just as a bolt of lightning struck the forest, splitting a tree in two and causing Celeste, Margot, Ginette, Sarah Rosenberg—and perhaps even Renée Lepine—to start in their beds.

Louise fell to the floor, her foot broken.

"Am I to suffer the same fate as my landlady? Oh, such a terrible curse!"

And deep within her, a dam broke and everything collapsed. The years—her years—came tumbling down on her head in huge chunks of ice, and she blacked out. Across the kitchen floorboards, the flame from the candle spread, circling her body like the halo of a spotlight. She was onstage at the Théâtre de l'Ambigu-Comique, her foot folded in thirds in a bucket of elephant dung, surrounded by hat-wearing men, their fingers pointed skywards, necks craned, in a doleful sarabande: "Louise, ah! Louis. Louise, ah! Louis," they called for her to come back to them, the Louise as they once knew her, a gloomier Sarah Bernhardt, a woman of anecdotes, a liar the likes of which you've never seen, on her head a paper crown and in her hand a sugar sceptre. The actress shaped like a playing card appeared by her side—her name, although no one knew it, was Dame Darquise Larocque—and hoisted her upright by the armpits, whispering a dangerous order in her ear: "Cut the foot off, cut it all, cut the leg off at the thigh, if you have to," but Louise was still asleep, eyes open, mouth wide, a black lake waiting to form the words that would either drown her or save her.

It was an enormous clap of thunder that resuscitated Louise Beurre, and a simple, involuntary movement that freed her foot from its rusty prison.

Each in their own homes, sitting by their windows, Celeste, Margot, Ginette, and Sarah Rosenberg stared as far into the distance as the storm would allow; they could all make out, somewhere beyond the trees, reflecting off the clouds in the gentle hues of daybreak, the flickering glimmer of a huge fire.

Louise Beurre had to join them, those women who watched and waited so anxiously. She leaned on the table and hobbled over to the window. Upon seeing the sky turn blood-red, it was she alone who realized the sordid drama that was playing out at Bella Webb's house. Bella, as voracious as a spider, crushing, strangling, and lacerating Renée Lepine, her Renée, "My Renée," thought Louise.

So perhaps she did see her through the sheets of grey rain, perhaps she did see her through her own tears of agony, her left foot *en pointe* like that of a Russian ballerina, but oh, she *did* see her, she swore she did, and would spend the rest of her days swearing she did to everyone, to Old Mr. Roux, to Basil, to the women, to Celeste, Margot, Ginette, to the police commissioners, to the investigators. She would shout herself hoarse, but no one would listen, because it would have been decided and proven beyond a doubt that no one had survived, and that the bodies of two women had been found in the burnt-out remains of the house; but Louise knew she'd seen her pass by the house: Bella Webb, more purple than the night, a large bag in her hand, fleeing the appalling scene, a charred beast seeking a lair where it could hide, burrow, bide its time, and gnaw its bones.

She wasn't dreaming anymore. Renée Lepine, stretched out beneath Bella Webb's farm, her nose emerging from the ground like a root. In the middle of a big bed of dirt, wedged between the child, the husband, the men—Bella's other sleepers. Renée Lepine who, right up to the final moment, was convinced she never dreamed, would forever sleep like a mummy, eyes wide, heart stopped; she dreamed no more.

QC FICTION

Current & Upcoming Books

01 *LIFE IN THE COURT OF MATANE*
by Eric Dupont
translated by Peter McCambridge

02 *THE UNKNOWN HUNTSMAN*
by Jean-Michel Fortier
translated by Katherine Hastings

03 *BROTHERS*
by David Clerson
translated by Katia Grubisic
Finalist, 2017 Governor General's Literary Award for Translation

04 *LISTENING FOR JUPITER*
by Pierre-Luc Landry
translated by Arielle Aaronson and Madeleine Stratford
Winner, 2017 Expozine Best Book Award

05 *I NEVER TALK ABOUT IT*
by Véronique Côté and Steve Gagnon
translated by 37 different translators

06 *BEHIND THE EYES WE MEET*
by Mélissa Verreault
translated by Arielle Aaronson

07 *SONGS FOR THE COLD OF HEART*
by Eric Dupont
translated by Peter McCambridge
Finalist, 2018 Scotiabank Giller Prize
Finalist, 2018 Governor General's Award for Translation

Printed by Imprimerie Gauvin
Gatineau, Québec